Colour me a Rainbow

Mala Rihan

Rita Chhablani

Jayashree Dhillon

Manjula Shukla

Shenaz Setna

VISHWAKARMA
PUBLICATIONS VP ™

Colour me a Rainbow

1ˢᵗ Edition - Published by Vishwakarma Publications in India in April 2017

© Author

ISBN - 978-93-85665-67-7

Published by:
Vishwakarma Publications
283, Budhawar Peth, Near City Post, Pune- 411 002.
Phone No: (020) 20261157
Email: info@vpindia.co.in Website: www.vpindia.co.in

Cover Design
Chaitali Nachnekar

Typeset and Layout
Gold Fish Graphics, Pune.

Foreword

There is a world of difference between feature films and advertising clips made for television. The former provides filmmakers a fair amount of 'elbow room' to lead the viewer by the hand in a particular direction towards a predetermined end. The latter needs to be pithy, to the point, attention grabbing and very concise, rarely exceeding 30 seconds.

This is the same challenge faced by short story writers when their work is compared to authors writing voluminous 400-600 page tomes peppered with rambling prose to 'build up' the atmosphere for an unsuspecting reader.

'Colour Me A Rainbow' is a collection of very readable short stories put together by a talented bunch of authors cast in the mould of literary advertising copywriters! The authors have admirably tackled the challenge of conveying so much without being verbose or resorting to unnecessary embellishments to 'dress up' their offering.

The reader remains invested in the story telling right through and, where required - as when the story trails off - is given the liberty to script a personalised ending as per one's imagination.

I wish to congratulate the amateur authors for giving us the opportunity to sample so many slices of everyday life through their efforts. I am sure that the collection will occupy an important place on the mantel shelves of collectors.

Happy reading!

Wg Cdr (Retd) Rakesh Sharma
Ashoka Chakra
First Indian Astronaut

Introduction

It all started with a small group of women invited to tea at Rita Chhablani's house on the 9th of Feb 2009. A member of a writers' group in Chicago, Rita was now in Pune and was keen to begin a similar group here.

She had selected friends and acquaintances who were very enthusiastic about writing. There was Kavita, Rita's quiet and gentle sister; Mala, confident with years of experience in writing and editing; Manjula, strong and silent but sharp as a razor; Shenaz, a friendly soul with her own special brand of humour and Jayashree, vocal and fond of descriptions.

After lengthy discussions over tea and biscuits, the group decided to meet fortnightly. And the 'Word Scriptors' group was born. They met with great regularity, armed with an article or story to be read out and critiqued by the rest of the group.

As the years went by, they evolved into a strong sisterhood with the writing of each member rising to a different level. The stories now came alive. They were written straight from the heart, each crafted to perfection, carrying a myriad of emotions, humour and pathos. The writers would chuckle, shake their heads, show concern, shed a tear or have a hearty rib-tickling laugh while reading the stories.

Over time, they felt a deep urge to share these treasures with a larger audience and so decided to publish this book. Their stories carry the flavour and spice of Rita's knotty tales, Manjula's mysteries, Jayashree's reminiscences, Shenaz's sparkling wit and Mala's musings.

As the Word Scriptors say,

"Our personalities and natures are different from each other, so are our styles and genres of writing." *Vive la différence!*

Enjoy dear reader!

CONTENTS

1

Nightfall in Nainital

Jayashree Dhillon

It was a dark, moonless night. A thick fog had enveloped the mountains and the valley. A lone army Jonga (army patrol vehicle) slowly drove up the narrow, deserted mountain road. Even the powerful, twin beams of the Jonga's headlights could not pierce through the wall of fog. 'A white-out,' Major Pradhan thought to himself, a term describing the poor visibility conditions, caused by heavy fog that descends on the mountains during winter nights. Visibility was almost zero. He couldn't see anything beyond a distance of a couple of feet.

Maj Pradhan was sitting in the front of the vehicle, beside his driver, who was struggling to move ahead in the dark. The major's wife and two kids sat at the back. They were on their way to Nainital and had started out from the small town of Joshimath that morning. Driving in that darkness was extremely dangerous, especially in that terrain. On one side of the road was the high, forest-covered mountainside and on the other, was a deep gorge, whose depth couldn't be seen even on a fog-free, moonlit night. Pradhan and his driver knew this, as they had traversed that road several times before, though mainly in broad day-light.

That particular day, was the first time Maj Pradhan had taken his family along. They had left Joshimath at 7.30 that morning and had expected to reach Nainital around 5 pm. the same evening. But frequent stops for tea and juice and snacks for the kids, an extended lunch break, plus two punctures, had set them back by several hours. It was 8 pm at night, they should have been close to Nainital by then but had no way of finding out. There were no lights from a wayside hamlet or tea-stall. There was no passing car, truck or bus, to ask for help or directions. Just the darkness and the impenetrable fog. You see, nobody drives at night in the mountains.

The major and his wife consulted each other—should they stay the night in the Jonga, by the roadside, out in the wilderness? At least till day break or till the fog lifted? But they both knew that it would be deathly cold. They were all tired and hungry. Their stock of food and water was alarmingly low. A sudden shiver went down Mrs Pradhan's spine. She thought about what the other wives in the Officer's Mess had told her, "Make sure you reach before sun-down. The mountain forests are dangerous with wild animals like wolves and hyenas. They are known to attack people and even carry away little children." There was even talk of small, mountain leopards lurking in the forests. The lady looked at her two little girls huddled in blankets beside her. Mercifully, they were asleep. The prospect of spending a night in the Jonga didn't appeal to her at all.

The couple took a decision. They would try and move ahead, no matter how slowly, towards Nainital instead of waiting any longer. Maj Pradhan picked up the powerful torch lying in the vehicle, switched it on and stepped out of the Jonga. Then he helped his wife out of the vehicle. Next, holding the torch in one hand, he held his wife's hand in his free hand and together they moved in front of the Jonga. They walked a few feet away, carefully taking one step after another. He turned around and called out to the driver to follow them. After every few steps, Pradhan would flash the torch at the stone culvert by the edge of the road, to make sure they remained on the right track. Any wrong move would have been fatal!

Progress was painfully slow. It seemed to take ages to move just a couple of feet. It was eerie to walk in the pool of light from the torch while darkness enveloped them from all sides. Sounds of night insects and the hooting of owls, added to their anxiety.

The couple trudged slowly for what seemed the longest half an hour. In fact, they had hardly covered any distance. Suddenly, they sensed the road turning on the side of the mountain. Was it a hair-pin bend?

As they turned along the mountain-side, Major and Mrs Pradhan saw a wondrous site! A few lights twinkled in the distance! The fog had also thinned considerably. With a great sense of relief, they scrambled back into the vehicle following them. Very slowly, but steadily, the driver covered the last few kilometres to the army mess located on the outskirts of Nainital, where they were to halt for the night. Though late, the mess staff were expecting them. Hot water, a hot meal, comfortable beds with thick army blankets and a crackling fire in the fire-place, awaited them.

Later that night, after Mrs Pradhan had tucked the blankets around the tiny forms of her little daughters, she turned towards her husband. Their eyes met and they smiled at each other. "We did it!" she exclaimed happily as she snuggled into her blankets.

2

The End of the Road

Manjula Shukla

It was not yet one o'clock. The air was still, the sky was heavily overcast with ominous clouds and a downpour could begin any moment. Naina would be back in another half hour or so, famished as usual and demanding food, the birthright of teenagers.

Radhika busied herself making preparations for lunch. The menu was *dosa, sambhar* and *chutney*. The *sambhar* was simmering in a pot and the aroma of fragrant spices was tickling the senses. The batter was ready and she put her heavy non-stick *tava* on the gas burner. On the other side of the kitchen counter she put coconut pieces in the mixer grinder for the *chutney*. Just then she heard the doorbell ring. Who could it be? Nobody was expected at this hour and Naina had her own latchkey.

Radhika peered through the peep hole and saw a shadowy figure. It was dark outside. The corridor lights should be put on at such times, she thought. Security must have screened the visitor if it was someone from outside the complex. With this comforting thought, she opened the door and was shell shocked. "Parag!?" burst out from her dry mouth.

This was her sister Avantika's husband, Parag. Avantika was much younger than Radhika and had been affectionately nicknamed Avani by her elder sister. Avani and Parag had got married three years earlier, both madly in love with each other. He had been the only son of doting parents from a rich business family. All had been well at first. A year into the marriage, recession had set in and the business had collapsed. Parag, a spoilt child at heart, couldn't handle it. He started drinking and gambling with whatever was left. His aged parents, deeply saddened by the behaviour of their son, relocated to their native lown, leaving the couple alone.

Avani, at her wit's end, had tried desperately to salvage their lives but was defeated by this hard blow of life. In front of her concerned family, she changed completely. She became a thin shadow of her former vivacious self. There were dark shadows under her eyes and her face acquired a haunted expression.

Once Radhika, had visited her unannounced and noticed a bruise on her left cheek. That had devastated her. She couldn't bear the thought of her beloved sister in an abusive relationship.

After consulting her parents and husband, she had spirited Avani out of the house to safety. That had been six months ago. Parag had raved and ranted but the family refused to reveal Avani's whereabouts. Divorce proceedings had been started. Radhika was extremely gratified to see her sister recovering, showered with love and care from the family, along with intensive counselling.

A sudden movement from Parag brought her back to the present moment. As Radhika was gathering her wits, he had already pushed the door open and was standing in the middle of the living room.

"How are you? I must observe social niceties, mustn't I? A public school education drills manners into you, like it or not. Nothing's changed here, I see," he said pleasantly, looking around. "Just a moment, is that another one of Naina's tennis trophies? Like mother, like daughter. You must be proud of her. Where are the others?" Without waiting for an answer, he peeped into each room, reassuring himself that there was nobody else at home. "Ah, my dear sister-in-law, I have a bone to pick with you. You ruined my life. You took Avani away from me and today I'm here to avenge myself," he said. Putting his hand in his trouser pocket, he took out a revolver and pointed it straight at Radhika's chest.

"Nothing to say now?" he taunted, murder in his eyes.

"You must be mad," burst out Radhika, horrified. "Are you still living in a make-believe world? Aren't you aware of reality?"

"What is reality?" he shot back "The fact is that I loved Avantika. I didn't let her meet her friends, family even you. I didn't let her go swimming even though she loved it. Do you know why? Because I wanted her with me all the time and you took her away from me. Yes! You, dear sister-in-law!" His face crumpled and tears glistened in his eyes.

"How I suffered when she left me, nobody understood." He paused and then continued in a tortured tone "I couldn't sleep nights without her. I have planned this for a long time, sis-in-law." With a fiendish gleam in his eyes, he said savagely, "It's the end of the road for me. I'm going to enjoy pulling the trigger. Let your husband, Samir, go through the same agony."

This couldn't be happening to her. Radhika wanted to pinch herself and wake up from this nightmare. There was a look of pure terror in her eyes. Her stomach was in knots and a feeling of intense dread gripped her heart. Her mouth felt bone dry and her hand involuntarily came up to wipe the sweat off her brow.

At the sudden movement, Parag gestured with the revolver. "No funny tricks, nothing can save you now."

'Take control, take control' from somewhere her mind was screaming at her. 'But how?' another part of her brain was asking. She got the answer in a flash of intuition, focus on his good looks.

From somewhere deep down, she dredged up a smile. "Come on, Parag. I can't believe you'd do such a thing. Avani would be so sad."

"Avani would be sad?" he pounced on her words. "I knew she loved me."

"Of course she did, she still does."

"Then why doesn't she come back to me?" Tears gathered in Parag's eyes. "No, you're lying to distract me. I know she has filed for divorce." There was a crazy look in his eyes as he said these words.

"Oh, Parag, you don't know the whole story," she said in soothing tones. "You'd be surprised at what is going on here."

"What? You have to tell me, please, please!" he said in changed tones.

From the corner of her eyes, Radhika saw the time. Heavens, Naina would be back in ten minutes or so. She had to think fast. "Let's have a cup of tea, shall we? Then we'll sit and talk comfortably. Of course, I just remembered, I have *dosa* batter ready. Would you like one?"

"I think I would," he said.

"Then come on into the kitchen. Avani has told me many times how much you love *dosas*. She used to joke that you could have it for breakfast, lunch and dinner. Just give me a moment and I'll have it ready."

She got up and went into the kitchen. Parag followed her and stood in the doorway. She lit the gas stove, dribbled oil on to the *tava* and busied herself adding condiments to the chutney.

All the while she kept up a cheerful chatter. "See, the batter is just right. You like the *sambhar* pungent, don't you? I know your tastes very well. The first time you came for dinner I had made *puris*, remember? It was only later that I got to know that you don't like them at all," she continued in a seemingly light hearted manner.

"For your wedding we had planned traditional food, but Avani told us to change the menu. By the way, do you know how handsome you were looking at the function?" Her intention was to stroke his ego and it worked. There was a pleased chuckle from him.

"Really? Nobody told me" he said.

"Avani should have told you, I'll tell her of this major lapse…" She continued in the same stream but her sharp ears were straining to hear her daughter Naina's footsteps.

"I'll never forget the scene when the *baraat* arrived and you got out of the car. Believe me, there were many girls who would have willingly changed places with Avani. Mansi was really envious and her other friend Aradhana, remember her? The tall fair one…"

There was a slight sound outside, that of a key being put in the lock. Only if someone was expecting it, would they have heard it. The key turned with a loud click and the door opened. Parag turned around with a loud exclamation "What the…"

This was the moment Radhika had been waiting for. Grabbing the heavy, heated *tava* with both hands, she swung it with all her might, a tennis champion's killing swing and hit Parag across the side of his temple. He collapsed on the floor with a loud cry of pain.

"Mom, what's wrong?" came Naina's frightened voice from the hall. Radhika fled out of the kitchen, caught her daughter's hand and dragged her out of the front door. "What are you doing?" Naina resisted and then saw her mother's terrified and frantic face.

In a split second she understood the urgency of the moment and ran with wings on her feet, Radhika behind her. As they ran out of the front door, Radhika had the presence of mind to pull it shut behind her and push the bolt home.

From within she heard a gunshot and realized Parag had taken the easy way out of the mess he had created. Her iron control broke and she started shivering so violently that she couldn't stand. Great shuddering sobs came from her throat as she collapsed on the staircase.

Clutching Naina close to her in a tight grip, she wept uncontrollably. She was weeping for the agony her sister had gone through, weeping for the wasted life of a person once very close to her and most of all weeping from the sheer relief of knowing that Naina and she were safe.

❏ ❏ ❏

3

Life Goes On...

Shenaz A. Setna

Noshir was managing, just about managing, without Shirin. He completed the crossword after breakfast, the same as always. Then, he did the household chores or went out to town on his twice a week marketing and outdoor tasks. After lunch he took a short siesta, attended to paperwork and watched television until tea-time. In the evening he would stroll down leisurely to the society clubhouse. There were always people to chat with there. Not that Noshir was a chatty type. Like most men, he kept himself to himself. However, he soon bonded with a few of his neighbours and took a few brisk rounds around the society walking track with Major Ahuja and a couple of other retired gentlemen.

He missed his wife Shirin in so many ways, but couldn't for the life of him express his emotions in words. "Life goes on," she had whispered to him as the end drew near. He remembered her, ever peaceful, dignified and accepting of the inevitable with a smile. He had thought at the time that she was referring to the future generations, their children and grandchildren. They were all precious to him. However, they lived at quite a distance from him and combined with their busy schedules and lifestyles, visited him less regularly than before. The house felt eerily empty and Noshir found himself alone and lonely quite often.

One sunny afternoon, after lunch, in the midst of an excruciatingly mind-numbing and boring television program, he turned his head and gazed at her chair. Shirin had loved that chair. It was big, comfortable and cozy, with an accompanying footstool to put one's feet upon and relax. She had inherited it from her grandmother and took great care of it, cleaning and polishing it regularly and getting the upholstery changed every time it looked dingy and worse for wear. He tried to imagine her sitting there, tried to focus on her face, but his brain would not co-operate. Instead, all he could remember was a sound, the definitive clickety-clack of her knitting needles. It was part of the rhythm of their daily lives.

The memories started rolling back; the basket full of balls of cream and buttercup-yellow soft wool and the pile of tiny garments that she had knitted during the months of her first pregnancy. They had been living up in the hills at that time, due to his work as the manager of a tea-estate, and she had been due to deliver in the first week of October.

"Our baby won't be able to wear all these clothes, even if they are worn just once!" he had exclaimed in amusement, teasing her.

She just smiled placidly. "Babies need lots of clothes," she had remarked and then proceeded to deliver twin baby girls a few weeks later.

The cream and yellow changed to pink and then blue, a few years later, when their son was born. She had knitted for Noshir too; big chunky sweaters that had kept him warm during the cold inclement winters, out on the hills. He still wore one or two of the lighter ones now, as well as the striped scarves and hats. The place and the seasons had changed and so had the garments. Life went on.

Noshir heaved himself out of the chair and went to look for Shirin's knitting basket. It was in its usual place, in the small cabinet close to her favourite chair. He became misty-eyed. He fished around until he found a sturdy pair of knitting needles and some dark wool. He instantly felt less lonely. Long ago, Shirin had taught him to knit during the long cold evenings and that shared activity had created a special and close bond between them.

He struggled for a while, trying to get the cast-on stitches to stay on the needles, but he was quite out of practice and they kept slipping off. The wool magically tried to tie itself into knots. Out of sheer irritation and desperation, he went onto the internet and found step-by-step instructions on the screen in front of him. He fetched the basket, needles and wool and settled himself in front of the screen. His eyes flew between the screen and the needles and wool, totally oblivious of the world around him.

This routine went on for a few days. He dropped stitches, put them back on, twisted and turned the wool around the needles in different shapes and ways, until he finally had a long scarf in front of him. It was uneven in breadth and texture, lumpy and bumpy, but still, he had created something. The clickety–clack of the needles had oddly given him a sense of peace and achievement and taken away some of the loneliness.

He practiced his knitting every afternoon, in front of the TV, and during the nights when sleep eluded him. He felt her presence in the room sometimes and felt less lonely, but he was still on his own.

His pile of scarves grew steadily. One day, as he was out on his errands, he noticed that the local school shop had a notice on the front door requesting clothes and other items for the poor children and orphans in their boarding section. He returned home and packed up all his scarves neatly, ready to take them to the shop the next day.

He was in luck. Plump, cheerful rosy-cheeked Ayesha Sharma was at the shop-counter, instead of the gaunt, cranky and irritable Sudha Shetty; more commonly referred to as Sourpuss by the local population. Ayesha was a drama and elocution teacher at the school and volunteered at the school-shop during her free time.

She beamed at him. Ayesha had been part of Shirin's large circle of friends and acquaintances. "Shirin made these?" she enquired in surprise, as she unpacked the parcel. "These will be very useful with winter around the corner."

"No," replied Noshir, bashfully, "I knitted them."

Ayesha was amazed and complimented him on his skills. She rummaged through her desk drawers and produced a leaflet, which she stuck under Noshir's large beaky Parsi nose. "You might be interested in this. It's for a good cause too. Think about it. Bye for now."

Noshir took the leaflet home and read it after dinner. It was about a project to knit warm clothes for babies and small children they had been placed in refugee camps, after a heavy deluge of rain and floods had displaced their families from their livelihoods, homes and villages, a couple of months ago. There was a picture of small infants swaddled in dirty torn newspaper to keep them clothed and warm. That was the part that made him cry. He remembered his children as infants, cute as buttons in their lovingly knitted woollies, protected from the chill of the cold mountain winters. He took out the basket again and made a mental list of how much more wool he would need to purchase and some knitting pattern books for babies on his next outing to town.

After his trip to the hosiery shop, he returned home and started to knit in earnest. Deciphering the instructions and somewhat complicated stitches required for the sweaters, kept him from brooding. He smiled to himself. "Imagine," he thought, "Noshir Bharucha—an elderly widower, knitting baby clothes," and chuckled to himself. He displayed every single finished item in front of Shirin's photo, for her approval and blessing. Her face and smile in the photograph, to him, seemed brighter and wider every day. His imagination was running riot, he grumbled to himself.

About two to three weeks later, Noshir took his little bundles to the school shop, fervently hoping that Ayesha would be there and not Sourpuss. Ah, he was in luck again. Ayesha was delighted and introduced him to the other members of the project committee over the next few days. His professional skills and business acumen were highly appreciated by them, and he was soon included in organizing events and raising funds for the project and school. Gradually, he made new friends and started socializing again. After a few months he realized that he enjoyed himself more, and was happier when Ayesha was around.

Ayesha was a Scrabble addict. Noshir liked the game and was quite proficient at it and had played it a lot with his children. Shirin, however, didn't like or play the game. Once Ayesha discovered that she would have a new, good Scrabble partner, she started popping in to Noshir's house with home-made cake, biscuits and snacks which they had with their tea, after their hour at the Scrabble board. She was a good cook, and encouraged him to cook simple, healthy meals, instead of depending on his temperamental cook, take-outs and junk food.

Life went on, just as Shirin said it would. Noshir and Ayesha kept their demons of loneliness and isolation at bay over cups of tea, cupcakes and the Scrabble board. Their friendship flowered and blossomed and they became each other's close companions and confidantes. Noshir looked at Shirin's photo every day and felt blessed. He was much happier than he had anticipated and he was content.

4

Bus No. 123

Mala Rihan

Menaka was standing at the bus stop, waiting for the bus no 123 to return from Tardeo where she worked, to her home in Colaba. It was her favorite ride and the best part of her day. After slogging at the desk for ten or more hours, she was returning home. Just thinking of it made her smile… a piping hot meal would be waiting for her. While she ate, she would enjoy mom's chatter, interspersed with terse comments from didi, her elder sister, Nirmala. Nikhil, her brother, would be in later. He would soon have them roaring with laughter, with his takes on the various people he met in the course of his day as a sales manager with Modi Xerox.

Ah, the bus! As always, she made a dash for the stairs and swiftly reached the upper deck, looking for the front seats, where the sea breezes refreshed her, and where she could see all the familiar sights. The sea never failed to enthrall her with its many faces… all familiar, yet ever new. Sometimes dark and swollen, sometimes calm and placid, sometimes frothy with shallow waves. As she glanced towards the promenade, she saw that as always, there were people everywhere; the walkers, the lovebirds, the vendors with their colorful balloons, decorations or fast food... what they called time pass...

Oh, bad luck! Today all the front seats were occupied and also the sea facing ones. She would have to spend her journey looking at all the dilapidated and rundown buildings along the road. They were impossible to maintain. Coats of paint held no sway against the sea breezes, the strong salty winds which blew here daily.

Determined to enjoy her end-of-day ride, Menaka looked to the left as the flyover ended and the buildings came into view. From the top of the double decker she could actually look into the houses. The bus lurched to a stop, and more passengers got on, none got off. People who travelled on buses rarely lived on the posh Marine Drive.

She looked up as the bus began again with a groan. And her blood ran cold. A strange drama was playing out. A man was strangling a woman in the first floor flat of a building right in front of her. His menacing figure arched above the woman who seemed very short. 'Was she seated?' wondered Menaka. She blinked, and the view changed. An old man was standing in his pajamas, in his balcony, grinning vacantly. Had she imagined it or was that scene so vividly etched in her mind, real?

Later as she walked home from the bus stop, her mind kept spinning around that instance, real or imagined. Dismissing the thoughts, she bounded up the stairs to their *barsaati*, the little one bedroom plus terrace that served as home to the four of them. For once, Menaka was silent, staring into space as mom chattered while making a cup of tea for her dear daughter.

"Whatever's the matter, *beti*?" She asked. "Did you have a bad day at work?"

As she herself was unsure of what she had seen, she told her mother nothing. Just smiled and made off with her tea to the terrace, brooding. Probably just my imagination, she thought. Though as a responsible adult and a staunch feminist, she should have been taking steps to help the poor lady she had seen.

"I'll make it a point to look at that flat tomorrow..." she decided before she finally fell asleep.

She woke up so late that she had to cab it to work the next morning. However, on the way back, next evening, Menaka was very tense. She didn't go up and occupy the front seat, which made the conductor, well aware of her preferences, give her a strange look.

Soon they had passed the flyover and approached the buildings. 'Which one was it? They all looked so similar. Oh there was the old man in his pajamas...' She'd missed it.

Next morning, she decided to go early to work. On the way, she got off at the bus stop near the place she had seen the incident. Walking up and down, she was unable to pinpoint the house. She gave up and squeezed into the next bus, reaching the clinic late.

That afternoon, a beautiful, well-dressed lady called Mrs. Gera walked in. She had a scarf around her neck and asked to meet Dr. Mehta, the gynecologist. As Menaka ushered her in, Mrs. Gera shut the door in her face!

'How rude!' She thought as she went back to her chair.

Once again in the evening, she took a window seat on the left of the bus, from where she could see into the buildings. Once again, she was not able to identify the flat that she had seen into earlier. She decided it was really none of her business and eased into the front seat that had just been vacated.

At the clinic, Mrs. Gera had become a frequent visitor. From once in a couple of months, she had started visiting the clinic every week. Yet she showed no signs of pregnancy. 'She doesn't seem to be pregnant and there are no tests. 'That is strange for someone visiting a gynaecologist,' thought Menaka. But Dr. Mehta was very strict about patient confidentiality and kept all her papers locked away. Anyway, she did most of her entries on the computer directly, unlike the other doctors who frequently asked Menaka to help make patient updates.

***

It was a cloudy Monday morning, with cool breezes bringing in the promise of rain.

"What a lovely day! How I would love to bunk and take a walk down Marine Drive," thought Menaka. But the clinic was always packed on Monday mornings. With a sigh, she collected her belongings and got off the 123 bus.

The morning passed in a blur of patients. Today most were for the ENT and pediatrician. Sneezing and coughing, the children huddled in the waiting room.

But here was Mrs. G. again in one more of her beautiful American chiffon saris. This time the scarf was wrapped around her face. As Menaka approached to call her in, Mrs. G. winced involuntarily and moved away from her with a shudder.

'Whatever was the matter with her?' she wondered.

When Dr. Mehta buzzed for assistance, she found the nurse had just sat down for a cup of hot tea... her first on this busy day. "I'll go," offered Menaka. As she walked into the clinic room, she almost broke out of her professional smile, seeing the patient's body. It was so heavily bruised. The left cheek had a big bruise too.

Dr Mehta frowned on seeing her. She knew Menaka was a good receptionist but she was young and perhaps, might talk. They attended to the patient in silence, and Menaka was pulled aside as Mrs. G was dressing.

"Not a word about this!" warned Dr Mehta.

So that was the reason for her frequent visits. What a sad thing to happen to a beautiful lady.

***

It was a couple of weeks later that Menaka happened to glance up from her mobile just as the bus was passing the same building. Omigod! There they were again! The same couple. This time, the woman was leaning out of the window screaming for help, and the man was standing behind her!

Shocked, Menaka looked at the conductor by her side who was also gaping at the scene. In a rare moment of clear thinking, they both grabbed the thin rope that clanged loudly in the driver's cabin, indicating that there were passengers who wished to get off. The bus came to a shuddering stop.

By this time, Menaka, the conductor and another young man had reached the lower deck and they jumped off the bus, running to the building. Samudra Mahal, Menaka's hyper alert mind noted as the trio ran up the stairs to the first floor flat. Luckily, the door was ajar and yielded to a push. The men grabbed the offender, wrestling him down to the floor, leaving Menaka to handle the lady.

"Are you hurt?" she asked, gently touching the woman on her shoulder.

And then she gasped! It was Mrs. Gera with another set of bruises on her and a black eye beginning to develop!

The police had been called by one of the passengers on the bus which was still at the kerb, waiting for the people to come back. As the police arrived, the conductor returned to his bus. Menaka felt obliged to stay. After all this was a patient.

Looking around the house, it was difficult to imagine that the exquisitely turned out Mrs. G. lived in such a mess. Broken crockery was strewn over the floor. The flat looked like it could do with much cleaning. Bare walls with peeling paint testified to the poverty of the people staying there.

Much confusion prevailed, the police becoming violent with the man who would not stay still even after being caught in the act.

"Please don't hurt him," croaked out Mrs. G. from her bruised lips. "He can't help his actions. He is a schizophrenic and doesn't know what he is doing."

The police were persuaded to let the matter drop. Dr. Mehta, responding to Menaka's frantic call, came in to treat and counsel Mrs G.

"Menaka, let me drop you home. It's really late." said Dr. Mehta. So Menaka sat in the car with the 'gynie' as they irreverently called her.

"Why doesn't she leave her husband, ma'am?" asked Menaka, badly shaken.

"My dear, this is not her husband. She left her husband shortly after marriage as he was abusive and unkind. This is her brother... And she is his only living relative. He lives alone, but whenever she visits in order to look after him, this is what he does."

"But can't she put him into some institution?"

"Unfortunately, that cannot be done unless he agrees. And he is too clever to behave like this in front of others. So he cannot be committed to an asylum."

Narrating this incident to her family after dinner, to explain why she had landed home so late, she looked around at her warm, sympathetic family, grateful for all they brought to her life.

"*Kismet!*" was her sister's simple comment and they could only nod in agreement.

❑ ❑ ❑

5

Good God, Godbole!

Rita Chhablani

Mumbai

Hitler Godbole... was that a name? Hitler Srikant Godbole...Why the hell had his parents given him a name like that? And the surname made it worse. His colleagues, all perverse, made fun of him all the time. And to be stuck with a short stocky frame with a bald patch on his head to boot, it was hell. No girl in the office looked at him or even gave him a second glance. Poor Godbole, they clucked their tongues with sympathy when they flitted by, seeing him, the humble typist clicking away at his innocuous typewriter. He was totally fed up, dejected, depressed.

One evening, after office, he got onto the bus at Flora Fountain at his usual bus stop but got off mid-way at Marine Drive. He clambered up the parapet, ready to jump into the grey, angry waves lashing the waterfront, wanting to get swallowed, get lost from the face of this earth, from his boring, useless, meaningless life. All of a sudden, the image of his greedy twin Stalin, flashed across his eyes. That rascal had usurped their huge ancestral property, in Delhi and lived in great style in their mansion in the posh suburb of Chanakyapuri. He travelled in style in his Mercedes, one among a burgeoning fleet of luxury cars, Buicks, and BMWs, that adorned his garage. He also owned the decades old, huge manufacturing plant of *paan masala* their parents had started. Taking advantage of his brother's naiveté, Stalin had usurped all the inheritance. Even the 16 bed-roomed mansion, that has been featured in a leading interior design magazine. That had really, really hurt.

Nostalgic memories flashed through Hitler's mind about this huge estate situated on top of the hill, overlooking the valley of Dehradun. The view was stunning. He remembered how his brother and he, during childhood, would shout out happily into the valley, with the mountain ranges reverberating with their echoes.

His parents had passed away when he was eighteen, leaving a treasure trove for their two sons, who could have lived and enjoyed the spoils equally in peaceful harmony and co-existence. Like a fool, he had trusted his brother and had given away his power of attorney.

Now here he was, a humble clerk, plodding away with heavy registers at work, tallying accounts honestly, not allowing a single rupee to make its way into either his own or other greedy pockets. What was the use, he thought, misty-eyed, ready to take the plunge, when he heard a voice from the distance, shouting desperately, "Godbole…"

His eyes darted around, as he stood on one leg, arms spread by his sides, in the famous Titanic pose. It was Anjali he saw, the bright new girl who had joined their legal section. She was not just a wow in the looks department but she was a champion in her fight for injustice, so he had heard on the office grapevine. And here she was, rushing towards him, looking at him with utmost concern in her eyes.

"What are you doing up there?" she asked. Godbole stared at her, mesmerized, as though she was an apparition.

"Come down, come down," she continued, stretching her hand towards him. "I have news for you, Godbole, Sir."

The word 'Sir' clinched it. No one had ever called him Sir and with such respect. He wavered, his leg behind, still suspended up in the air. Suddenly, something within him stirred and he brought his leg down and steadied himself, held the hand she had extended, feeling its softness. It was the first time he had ever touched a woman and it sent shivers running down his spine. It was a strange feeling, but felt good. Lost in pleasant thoughts, he stood beside her, now on firm ground.

"Sir," Anjali's voice brought him back from his pleasant reveries. "I was in the bus going home when I saw you...," standing on that parapet... I pulled the bell and rushed out...

No human being had ever shown such care and concern in his existence. Godbole, unused to such attention, could not control his emotions any longer and burst into tears, knowing it was unmanly, but he did not care.

"Sir, I am sorry...did I say anything that offended you?" stuttered the baffled girl.

Godbole stopped crying at once. "You offend me? No... you are much too kind, the first ever human being... who has cared for a nobody like me."

Soon, they were sitting on the bench, unaware of the sound and fury of the lashing waves, sipping away at tender coconut water she had so thoughtfully bought from a passing coconut vendor.

"Oh, Sir... I forgot. This document came for you as soon as you left this evening," she said, pulling out a white envelope from her purse and flourishing it at him. "It seems to be a legal document. Maybe you should open it!" she suggested, when she saw him push it into his shirt pocket.

Not wanting to displease his new friend and well-wisher, he took out the envelope and looked at it. He began wondering when he read the name of the sender. It was from a lawyer. When he read the contents he jumped up and broke into a comical jig.

With disbelief, Anjali stared at him, wondering what had got into the man, who was such a recluse otherwise and the butt of ridicule in the office. A champion for the underdogs, she had many a time fought with her colleagues over their unreasonable and cruel attitude toward him, but to no avail.

"I am rich... I am rich... beyond compare. My aunt, she was a single woman, has left me with her fortune," he screamed at the top of his voice.

This sweet, simple man looked so comical that Anjali could not help herself and burst into peals of laughter.

Godbole suddenly stopped and came and sat down by her side. "You know, you are the first person in my life who has given me a few moments of her time. For that I am deeply grateful and I must reward you for that," he said softly looking at her. Quietly, he pulled out the pen from his pocket and scribbled a few words on the document. Handing it to her, he said, "This inheritance is of no use to a useless man like me, a person that the world does not like, does not want. I bequeath it all to you, my angel."

Speechless, Anjali looked at him.

Godbole stood up. His feet broke into a jig again. This time it was like a Red Indian war dance, with cries like, 'Whoopee!' Like he had gone mad, lost it.

Before Anjali could comprehend what was happening she saw him run and climb the parapet once again. She let out a cry, "Stop, Sir... be careful!" she screamed and held her breath when she saw a huge grey monsoon wave rise and then slowly subside. And then there was nothing. Godbole, the sweet simple man was no longer there. The parapet was empty. The wave had swallowed him.

Tears striped Anjali's cheeks as she stood thinking of this man. He had first caught her attention when she had seen a short stocky man helping an old blind woman cross the road. She had inquired, but colleagues had mocked at him. She had often seen him giving away his entire meal to beggars, sitting in front of the temple across the street from the office. The world had lost a good, kind human being.

She sighed and turned to go to the empty bench, to sit and collect her thoughts, when her eyes fell on the legal paper still lying there. He had signed away his entire inheritance to her, just like that! Who would do that! She was about to tear it when she heard a voice. "Don't waste your tears on me, angel," and Godbole, like a Jack in the box, appeared from behind the very bench she was seated.

"You alive! Here!" she exclaimed.

"I had every plan to die but fell down and had a miraculous escape," said Godbole. "You were so busy crying, you did not see me sneaking back. I could not die, especially now after meeting you."

"You have always reminded me of Robin Hood," said Anjali with a smile. "Thank God, you are alive!"

***

A month later

The company Godbole worked for was bought out. The shocked employees stared at the new board: Godbole, Anjali and Associates.

In his newly acquired mansion, Godbole and Anjali picked up their glasses of champagne, held them high and brought them together in a toast. The clinking of crystal was like music to his ears. "Cheers to my angel," said Godbole.

"Cheers to the kindest man on this earth," shot back Anjali spontaneously.

After a sumptuous dinner, Anjali was ready to leave.

Back home, as Anjali basked in the comfort of her soft silk comforter she was able to afford now, her thoughts went to Godbole. Appearances were so deceptive. He was no Hitler. The man had a heart of gold. Here was a man who expected nothing out of her. Theirs was friendship bonded by respect and affection.

There were no strings attached. There was one difference, though. He was no longer Hitler.

Now she called him Srikant! The whole office did!

'They'd better!' She smiled.

6

A Shakespearean Drama

Manjula Shukla

"Ma, I'm really bored, the holidays seem to be going on forever. I think I'll read some of Shakespeare's plays. I really enjoyed Julius Caesar in the tenth grade," were the words spoken aloud one bright, sunny morning.

'Good,' I thought, 'that will keep her out of my hair.' The 'her' in question was my fifteen year old daughter, Bela, at a loose end just after her board exams. With short curly hair and flashing eyes, she was a perfect example of the tempestuous teen. Bela could complicate a simple situation beyond imagination and then extricate herself neatly with a winning smile. I was finding my hands rather full with both the kids home after the exams. My nerves were shot to pieces keeping them occupied and entertained. Thankfully, Sumit, the elder by two years, was more sensible and mature and I could count on his support.

"A wonderful idea," I enthused "we have the complete works of Shakespeare. You can get started right away." Little did I know what was in store for us.

The next morning I was busy in the kitchen, preparing for the arrival of my nephew and niece from Bombay. They were to spend a week of their holidays with us. We were all looking forward to it.

"Oh Ma, Ma, wherefore art thou Ma?" a soulful voice trilled melodiously. 'So it's *Romeo and Juliet* at the moment' I thought.

"In the kitchen," I answered. She appeared at the doorway in a second.

"When doth my kith and kin arrive?" she asked plaintively.

"Now wait a moment, where's that from?" I asked suspiciously.

"Oh Ma, you think I'm incapable of speaking old English on my own, do you?" she sniffed, tossed her head and flounced out. She seemed to have been well and truly bitten by the Shakespearean bug.

The much awaited guests arrived in the evening. After a joyous reunion of cousins, the children disappeared into their rooms. Suddenly Bela appeared in the drawing room followed by her cousin, Antara. There was an exquisite cut-glass figurine in her hand.

"*Masi*, I got this for *didi*," said Antara handing it to me. "Oh, that's beautiful. Let me have a look," I said. While I was admiring the gift and trying to see the light break up into rainbow colours as it passed through, Antara took a step forward, caught her foot in the floor rug and slipped. She was able to regain her balance but her elbow jostled my hand, the figurine fell on the floor and shattered into a thousand pieces.

"You block, you stone, you worse than senseless thing," stormed Bela, as enraged as Flavius, at the common citizens of Rome.

"Hush, hush child, it was an accident. Antara, don't cry. Bela, tell her it's all right," I tried to make peace.

"The quality of mercy is not strained. It droppeth as the gentle rain from heaven above upon the place beneath. It is twice blest. It blesseth him that gives and him that takes. I

Forgive Thee," with a flourish and a suitable exit, Bela left as regally as Portia from the court of Venice, leaving me to pick up the pieces and wipe Antara's tears.

"Let's go for a picnic," the kids clamoured the next day. "Where would you like to go? The adventure park? Trekking? Boating?" I asked.

Bela was not participating in the discussion. She was sitting dreamily on the settee with a faraway look in her eyes.

"I know a bank where the wild thyme grows, where oxslips and the nodding violet grows…" she said, lost in visions of midsummer nights.

"Shut up Bela, what is this about banks? We want to go for a picnic, not the HDFC bank round the corner," said Sumit in a scathing tone. "Mom, what's wrong with this girl?"

Just then the doorbell rang. Akshay my nephew opened the door. An elderly couple stood outside.

"My name is Amar Patel and this is my wife, Vandana. We are your next door neighbours. We're just moving in," they introduced themselves.

"Welcome to our housing society. Please come in. Children, meet Aunty and Uncle," I said.

"What are your names?" the gentleman asked in kindly tones. The kids answered in a kind of roll-call.

"Sumit"

"Akshay"

"Antara"

And then "What's in a name? A rose by any name would smell as sweet. However, for thy convenience, thou canst address me as Bella."

"What is this now? Does she think she's Isabella or Arabella?" I wondered. Sumit gave the guests a significant look and tapped his forehead.

"Mr. Patel, do you need any help? You must be busy getting things in place. Boys, go and help Aunty and Uncle, girls come and help me prepare a snack for them," I broke up the uneasy gathering.

"Thou art not just; thou art biased against the fairer sex, however, thy will shall be done," delivering these words in a raging tone, Bela stormed into the kitchen prepared to do her worst.

Later on in the day we went for a picnic to a water park nearby. The children enjoyed themselves tremendously. They went on every ride more than once and still queued up for more. The more dangerous the ride, the more the kids enjoyed themselves. Thankfully Bela even forget Shakespeare, except for the time when she asked for wine cakes and ale for refreshment.

"Ma, I'm getting tired of Shakespeare. I think I'll read Daphne Du Maurier now," she said the next day.

"Thank God for that," I thought. But wait a minute, what's this?

Bela sat on her bed, hugging her pillow, staring dreamily into space. "I can just visualize it, the never ending Cornish shore, waves on the horizon, the stormy seas, the lashing rain, daring smugglers, casks of whiskey, ship wrecks, Jamaica Inn…" she trailed off.

"Oh heavens," I thought in a panic, "How will we cope with that?"

7

Off with the Old and on with the New

Shenaz A. Setna

" I like this book—it works for me, the way Laila makes up her mind and sticks to her decisions, in spite of her family's opposition..." Preeti's opinion was abruptly cut off as her friend Anna put up her hand to prevent her continuing.

"Sorry Preeti but that was last month's book. And you said you didn't like it then!"

Preeti flushed red in embarrassment, looked down for a few seconds and then squeaked out, "Did I?"

"Yes you did! I remember!" said Sharmin.

"Have you actually read it?" asked Farida with a sad shake of the head, raised eyebrows and a look on her face that expressed her confidence that Preeti hadn't actually done so.

Preeti looked at the book which was on the table in front of her and opened it. Her name and the date she had bought it were scrawled hastily in pencil on the first page. 'That's what widowhood does to a woman,' she thought. 'To put your name and date on everything to remind yourself of who you are, a single person, not part of a couple any more, reminding yourself that you are still alive as days go by, getting on with the daily routine of life.'

She remembered that she had to buy and send out a fresh set of New year cards, because she had signed the first batch with "Love and best wishes from Ravi and Preeti," as she had quite forgotten that Ravi's ashes had been scattered amongst the sand dunes, close to his favourite hang-out just outside the city limits, barely a few months ago.

Preeti got up a little unsteadily from her chair, put her hands on the table to steady herself for a few seconds, picked up her handbag, and said in a slightly shrill wobbly voice, "Will be back in a jiffy, off to the Ladies—too much coffee!"

She sighed again, could her friends tell that she wasn't enjoying the book club meetings as she used to? That going to bookshops, browsing through stacks and shelves of magazines and books and bringing them home didn't thrill her anymore? And that she was not only concerned about it but hated herself a bit for it?

Preeti walked slowly towards the rest-rooms, her high heels click-clacking on the tiled floor of the coffee shop. As she passed the cashier, he looked up at her pale face and asked, "Are you ok, madam?" She nodded at him in assent, but the old man shook his head sadly as she passed him by. She noticed that her legs were shaking slightly and she felt a bit unsteady on her feet, and so she leaned on a pillar for support. She closed her eyes and said a little prayer. She felt better a few seconds later, and was about to open her eyes, when Laila's voice wafted past her ears.

"Of course, it's been nearly a year now; I don't think she'll stay much longer, not now…"

"That Ravi's dead" Anna finished the sentence in her cold flat voice. Had it always irritated her that Anna loved to interrupt people and finish their sentences? "Ravi didn't let her out of his sight when they were together, did he?" Sharmin piped in.

Actually it was the other way around. Preeti couldn't trust him around wine or women but the rage, tears and words remained stuck in her throat.

"No he didn't," said Farida, not as loud as the others, but loud enough for her to hear. "I don't think she's going to function well here without him, her mind isn't even on the book-club, let alone their business. She'll be off before you can say…" "Abracadabra!" popped in Anna again in a fake Arabic accent, another trait that annoyed Preeti quite a bit.

They had all been living in Dubai long enough to learn the local language, but none of them had bothered to make the effort except for herself. Her daily and then weekly language lessons with her neighbor, Mrs Bassaam, who was also a school teacher, had given her not only a basic, but more than adequate command over the local language. "I only need to know the words, *Wahed gaiser*"–more wine," Ravi had sneered at her. Ironically, it was the ever flowing supply and intake of alcohol that turned his liver into mush and eventually did him in.

The voices continued. "Of course now, she's footloose and single and between us girls, my husband Shahpur has always fancied her," Anna not to be outdone, exclaimed "Mine too! Ugh!" "Maybe because she's such a quiet little mouse!" said Sharmin with a snigger. "The men want to know what will make her squeal!" Loud sniggers, titters and giggles followed.

At that point, Preeti somehow found the strength within her to detach herself from the pillar and walk towards the rest-room. She splashed her face with water to refresh herself and stared at her reflection in the mirror. A mouse? Is that what her friends thought of her? She knew that eaves-droppers rarely heard good about themselves, but the malicious gossip had unleashed her inner courage and character. She touched up her make-up, brushed out her hair and looked at herself critically in the full-length mirror. Not bad for 30, she mused. Her only condition to start a family was for Ravi to stop his endless drinking, which had stopped, unfortunately, permanently. She missed him, the Ravi she first knew, not the alcoholic he had transformed into.

When Ravi had been in the hospital, with the drips, tubes and monitors attached to every part of him, he had caught her hand and whispered to her, "I think you should go back to Mumbai, if anything happens to me." "Why?" she had asked immediately, thankful for the dim lighting that covered up the flush of red on her face. This was the result of her guilt, arising from the lack of reassurance and affection shown by her to Ravi. She knew enough Arabic to understand the local medical staff as well as the Indian doctors' conversations and had realized that things were not going to get better.

"Because handling the business here is very tricky and being a single woman here will make it more difficult, almost impossible. You'll be near your brother and your relatives in Mumbai." She didn't have the heart to remind him that she and her brother had never really got along well and she wasn't on friendly terms with his wife or family.

She remembered her sense of relief shortly after he had passed away. She had realized that she was finally free of the constant verbal, emotional and physical trauma that she had been subjected to by Ravi's abusive behaviour and had finally been liberated from it. His death had however left her with wildly conflicting emotions of insecurity, fear and vulnerability, accompanied by occasional bouts of peace, contentment and hope, garnished with a hefty dose of guilt.

She heard the restroom door open with a clatter and shook herself out of her reverie. She knew that the time had come to make a clean break with all the negative portions of her past and to march ahead confidently into the future. She squared her shoulders and walked back slowly to the table, but didn't sit down on the chair.

"My, my! Where did you disappear to for so long?" questioned Sharmin with raised eyebrows. "We finished our book review and our coffee and were wondering whether to send a search party out for you. We are ordering lunch now and choosing a book and a date for our next meeting."

"I don't think I'll have time for the book club next month" said Preeti in the calmest tone she could muster. "Ah!" Anna exclaimed with a smug smile on her face and looked her up and down in a patronizing fashion. "I have things to do and will be very busy for some time. Bye!" Preeti turned to leave and reached the door but halted for a few seconds to make a quick call and then to let a mother with a child in a stroller to pass through before her. It was long enough to hear her friends' chatter again.

"She may be putting her house on the market then!" Sharmin's voice floated through to her ears followed by Farida's sympathetic voice. "Or she may be packing up and going back home to Mumbai. None of us thought that any one of us would become widows when we came out here, did we?"

'Yes', Preeti thought sadly, in agreement, 'We all believed we would live happily ever after.'

She took a step forward, then stopped short suddenly, turned and went back to the table and announced, "I'm not going back—I'm staying! I'll keep in touch; I will send you an invitation when everything is finalized!" She paused long enough to see the astonished expressions on their faces and for once Anna was dumb-founded with her mouth round and open like a gasping goldfish.

Farida was the first to recover. "Invitation? For what?" she asked her.

Preeti smiled, "You'll know when you receive it. Bye! Ciao!" She turned around and walked out of the coffee shop abit lightheaded with freedom. She was neither indecisive nor lost but was imbued instead with a strong sense of purpose and vision for the future. She could finally do what she had always wanted to do. She felt the last few dismal years slip off her like a cloak.

She walked out onto the footpath, whilst making a mental list in her head. She would sell their share in the business to their Arab partner who she suspected had long been cheating them out of their rightful share of the profits. Next she would move into a smaller but more convenient apartment. The numerous boxes and bags stacked in the spare bedroom were filled with her finds, accumulated whilst wandering around the local markets and souks. They could be now unpacked in peace without fear of Ravi's snide comments and occasional and deliberate destruction.

Her language teacher, Mrs. Bassam, had acquired another student, a Canadian banker, a few months ago. He was very knowledgeable and passionate about art and antiques and was planning to open an art gallery in his home-town after he returned from his working stint in Dubai. They had sat over endless cups of coffee after their lessons, discussed their latest purchases and then progressed to personal plans for their future. Their chats were like rays of sunshine in her otherwise tense and murky days.

As she turned around the corner, she felt like the heroine, in the book, Laila, who made her decisions and stuck to them despite opposition. A few steps later, her cell phone trilled in a very special and distinctive ring tone. She answered it with a smile on her face, a sparkle in her eyes and looked up across the road to where a tall blond man was standing by the side of a car, smiling and waiting for her. She waved and smiled back at him, crossed the road and the expression in her eyes as she met him spoke louder than words. The look of surprised delight on his face made her heart beat a little faster. Her new life had begun!

❑ ❑ ❑

8

The Rajkumari's Secret

Jayashree Dhillon

They had been driving for a couple of hours in the scorching heat. The road was bad, broken in many places and pot-holed. It was a dry, forested area. They were anxious to reach their destination before night-fall. The trees threw lengthening shadows across the narrow, dusty road. Soon it would be dusk.

There were four young people in the car. Two couples. Rohit and his wife Neha and their friends, Akshay and his wife Preeti. They were on a holiday and had booked themselves for a night at a fort, which was converted into a hotel, a few years ago.

A few kilometres more of that bumpy drive and they suddenly came upon a battered board announcing the well-known game sanctuary. "Oh great!" Rohit, the man at the wheel exclaimed with obvious relief. "Considering the road, we should be at the fort in less than an hour!" The two girls sitting in the back-seat, had exhausted all their conversation and nodded off to catch a nap. They opened their eyes to look at the man who was driving and almost immediately closed them, to continue their snooze.

They drove in silence for about half-an-hour. The powerful car devoured the kilometres, till they saw a narrow road turning left from the main road. An old, faded, tin board, in barely legible letters, said 'Qila Padmapur.'

"Almost there now!" said Akshay, the man next to Rohit.

The light was fading. The narrow road had fields on either side. The landscape had changed completely. Unlike the dry and brown forest, the fields were lush and green. Ten minutes later, they drove past a small village, a cluster of about thirty huts. They could then clearly see the hill fort, looming in the distance. It was perched atop a hill, rising high above the flat terrain. They left the village behind and within minutes, they were at the foot of the fort. The two tired couples, stumbled out of the car and looked up in awe at the imposing, high ramparts of the 14th century fort. Solid, stone steps led to a massive, heavy wooden door.

"How do we get in?" "Can't we take the car inside the fort?" "What about our luggage?" the couples asked each other. An old watchman walked up to them. He was tall and well-built, had a salt and pepper beard and wore a colourful turban. He had heard their queries and after greeting them with a *'namaste'* (Indian greeting) and with an amused look in his eyes, he said that the car could not go inside. He then explained that the doorway, though massive, was just wide enough for an elephant to pass through. "In the old days, the maharaja and his family sat in a *houda* on top of the elephant, while the animal climbed on the wide, stone steps and led the procession into the fort," he added.

The watchman told the visitors that they would have to tackle the steep, stone steps and to make their climb easier, there was a thick rope nailed into the stone, side wall of the fort. The old man added that the hotel staff would carry their bags to their rooms.

In spite of that rope, the climb inside the fort was a great deal of effort for the young city dwellers. Puffing and panting, they entered. Once inside, they saw a beautiful sight! There was a large open area, a clearing, converted into a lovely garden. Flowering trees and shrubs adorned the garden and masses of brilliantly coloured bougainvillea, cascaded down from trees, arches and pillars. All around the garden, halls and lounges were designed, in traditional Indian style, to cater to the dining and leisure needs of the guests. The rooms were grandiosely called *durbars*, *mahals* and *baithaks*. The hotel staff too, were all in traditional attire.

On one side of the garden, tea was laid out. A steward led the two couples to a large table and handed them plates, to help themselves to a variety of tea-time snacks. The youngsters were hungry and were thrilled at the sight of cucumber sandwiches, piping hot *samosas*, pastries and thick slices of fruit cake. A waiter poured fragrant tea, into delicate china cups.

After that sumptuous tea, the two couples, Rohit and Neha and Akshay and Preeti, asked to be shown to their rooms. The living areas were in the upper floors of the fort. Narrow stone stairs led to the rooms, terraces and walkways. These were protected by solid stone ramparts, all around the fort. The couples, again had to grapple with a thick rope, strung through iron rings, embedded into the side wall of the fort. They hauled themselves up the steep stairs, one step at a time. The stairs had no railings and no bannisters. Well, it was a 14th century fort after all!

Tackling the steep steps, Neha muttered, "Doesn't this seem a bit strange? I feel uncomfortable climbing stairs so steep and with no railings to hang on to for support…"

"Of course not, babes! Nothing strange here," Rohit, her husband was quick to answer. "After all, it is an ancient fort.

We've never stayed in one before. Akshay booked us here for a different experience, remember?"

"It's not that…" Neha replied lamely. "It seems so, so isolated… almost eerie."

Preeti, who was clambering up behind Neha, added, "Yes, and isn't it strange that we didn't see any other hotel guests? Is it just the four of us in the entire place ?"

Akshay, Preeti's husband, was the last one on the stairs. "Oh, don't worry girls! The staff is all there. Besides, the manager told me that they were expecting a group of foreigners later in the evening. A group of ten guests. It's a regular hotel."

"Well, there's nobody here yet," Neha said, a bit anxiously.

Suddenly, a homing pigeon, flew into the turret above them, flapping its wings noisily. All four of them were startled and stopped in their tracks. "It's only a pigeon," the bell-boy waiting for them at the top of the stairs, said nonchalantly. "There are many pigeons here. They live in the walls and turrets of the fort. No need to be afraid," he added.

Finally, after a strenuous climb, the couples reached the terraces in front of their rooms. There were two of them adjoining each other. The couples were given a suite of rooms at the far ends of each terrace. "We have no room service but we will serve the morning tea here," the bell-boy pointed to the wrought- iron chairs and table arranged outside.

The couples looked around them. They were standing high up, on top of the fort. In the deepening darkness, they could see many terraces, one leading to another and all adjacent to the ramparts. A narrow stone walkway, ran alongside the walls. Small and large openings were present in the fort walls, presumably for shooting rifles and cannons! For miles around, there were the fields, with an occasional light glinting from the village below. Soon it was dark. An inky sky, pierced by a myriad stars, gave the place an ethereal feel.

The bell-boy opened their rooms and switched on the lights. A murmur of appreciation went up from the couples. The rooms were tastefully done up in vibrant colours. In the middle of the room, stood an old fashioned, four poster bed. The bed, tables, chairs and mirror frames were made of dark wood and designed to look like antique pieces. The quilts, tablecloths, curtains and cushion covers were in colourful prints. They felt they had stepped back into time and entered an ancient *haveli!* Yet, the rooms boasted of every modern amenity. There were fans and air-conditioners in every room. The bathrooms had running water, both hot and cold. A small table displayed a collection of bath and beauty products for the guest's convenience. The bell-boy showed them around the rooms and then said, "If you need anything, please ring for us. The bell is right here. Dinner will be served in the garden below, till 10 pm." He turned to go and then quickly disappeared down the dark, narrow stairs.

After a quick wash and change, the two couples cautiously climbed down the stairs leading to the garden. Dinner was already laid out on a long table, covered with a crisp, white table-cloth. Fine crockery and gleaming cutlery was arranged on it. Strategically placed candles cast flickering shadows to add to the pleasing atmosphere. Strains of soft, light Hindustani classical music could be heard in the background. The air was heavy with the aroma of rich, spicy food. An occasional breeze carried the scent of flowers across the garden.

A puppet show was going on at the far end of the garden. They, especially the girls, were relieved to see that the other group of hotel guests had arrived. The group, mostly foreigners, were watching the puppet show. Snatches of their conversation and laughter could be heard in the dining area. Knowing that there were other guests staying there, the youngsters didn't feel quite so alone after all.

Dinner was a pleasant experience. A selection of delicious dishes, served by courteous, well-trained staff, left the young guests happy and satiated. After a great meal, they moved to the open, garden area to enjoy their post dinner coffee. The group of foreign guests, probably tired after a long journey, had retired to their rooms, one by one. The puppeteer had collected his puppets and left. The folk-singers too, had ended their performance for the night. They were gathering their instruments before leaving. Only an odd staffer or two remained to clear up the ash-trays and glasses left around by the guests.

The two couples continued to sit in the garden. They'd had a wonderful evening and seemed reluctant to leave. It was late and getting a bit cold. Neha shivered and said, "I wish I had got my stole down from the room."

"It's getting late. Let's go up to our rooms now and catch a good night's rest," said Rohit. "If we wake up early enough, we can put in a bit of sight-seeing after breakfast. I believe there are a few spots of tourist interest around the fort. We also have a long drive back home tomorrow," he added.

The foursome got up to climb the arduous steps to their rooms, again. After the pleasant evening with good food, people, lights and music, the fort suddenly seemed very quiet. The music and the garden lights were switched off and the last few members of the staff had left for their quarters. All was silent and dark. The couples felt very alone. Small lights on top of the stairs, cast a dull, yellow haze, just about enough to see where they were stepping.

On the terrace, the same dull, yellow haze surrounded them. They could barely make out the parapet walls and the dark, solid ramparts of the fort. All around the fort were the fields. So lush and green in the day but in complete darkness at that time of the night. And above them was the inky sky, pierced by those stars that dared to shine through. In that total silence, their own voices sounded so loud that they started talking in low tones. Neha shivered again. The darkness and the uneasy feeling was getting to them. Without any further conversation, the friends wished each other "Good night" and went into their respective suites.

Switching on the lights changed the atmosphere. The pretty rooms improved their mood. In the next ten minutes, Rohit had changed, said, "Good night, babes," to his wife and flopped on to the bed. Within minutes, he was fast asleep and snoring gently. Neha changed into a pretty gown, combed her long hair and looked into the mirror to cream her face. Why did she feel that someone was watching her? On an impulse, she drew the curtains of every window, small and large, around her room.

Neha switched off the lights and almost ran to the bed. She got in quickly under the cosy quilt and cuddled against her husband's sleeping form. She felt better. She was tired but sleep evaded her. 'What was this strange, uneasy feeling?' she thought to herself. Her mind was tossing about with a thousand thoughts. 'Who were the people who lived here centuries ago? What was their life like? Had there been any battles around the fort? There must have been bloodshed. Were the women happy? Were they in *purdah?* Were they allowed to learn to read and write; to learn the arts, sword-fighting and horse-riding? Or were they shut in the women's quarters, left to cook and clean and amuse themselves?'

A bird suddenly flapped its wings noisily, disturbing the silence of the night. Neha was startled and felt scared. What disturbed that bird? Wait. Did she hear light footsteps outside on the terrace? Then she heard the tinkling of anklets. Her ears strained to hear the sounds. Who could it be? She knew her friend Preeti wore silver anklets all the time. But Preeti outside at this time? She shivered. She didn't have the nerve to go and look outside. She heard another set of footsteps. Heavier and firm. Were they a man's? Then she heard voices, a man's and a woman's. Talking in whispers, in soft, loving tones. A muted, dull light moved outside Neha's curtained glass door. She distinctly got a whiff of the fragrance of roses. Neha went cold. 'What was happening? Was she imagining all this? Or was this a dream?'

She was very scared and huddled closer to her husband. Rohit just groaned and went back to his snoring. Should she wake him up? What would she say to him? He was so fast asleep after three large whiskeys and that heavy meal. Neha was now feeling hot under the quilt. Her forehead was hot and sweaty. She covered her face to shut out the thoughts in her mind but it was no use. Neha couldn't sleep all night. She tossed and turned and it was only several hours later, when dawn was breaking that she slipped into a fitful sleep.

There was a distinct knock on the door. Neha, fast asleep, didn't even hear it. There it was again, a purposeful knock. It woke up Rohit, who sleepily stumbled out of bed to answer it. He opened the door to see a waiter. "Good morning, Sir. Your tea. I have laid it out on the terrace. Please ring if you want some more. Breakfast will be served till 10 am in the banquet hall down stairs."

"What time is it?" asked Rohit, rubbing his eyes sleepily.

"Seven o'clock, Sir," replied the waiter.

Rohit thanked the waiter and stepped out of his room. It was a beautiful morning. Not a cloud in the sky. It was pleasantly cool. There was a slight breeze. His friends Preeti and Akshay were already outside their room having their tea. They waved to him. Akshay called out, "Get up, sleepy heads. Tea is served. Come soon, before we polish off the yummy cookies."

"Just coming," Rohit waved back and answered his friends before turning to go into his room to wake up Neha. Neha was fast asleep, but had a troubled expression on her face, as if she had had a bad dream. Rohit shook his wife's shoulder gently, "Wake up sweetheart! Tea is served. Our friends are already up, enjoying their tea on the terrace."

Neha woke up, a bit disoriented, as if she didn't know where she was. Her mind was fuzzy. She hadn't slept well at all. The events of the night seemed so real to her. The thoughts were so real. Then the sounds? Had she imagined them? Or was it a bad dream? "You carry on Rohit. I'll join you in a few minutes," said Neha, her head still heavy.

Minutes later she joined her friends for tea. "Hello sleeping beauty," Akshay teased. "Slept well?"

"No, not at all," said Neha, stifling a yawn. She was in no mood to discuss her disturbing night with her friends.

Preeti persisted. "You look tired. What happened? Bad dreams?" she asked gently.

In spite of not wanting to, Neha soon shared the night's experience with her friends. They fell silent and let her do the talking. They all seemed concerned that Neha had heard footsteps, the sounds of a woman's anklets and even a man and a woman talking. They tried to lighten her mood by saying, "It must have been a bad dream. You were tired. These high stone walls, the solid ramparts and deserted terraces and walkways must have got to you. We know you have a vivid imagination!"

"No, no, no. I definitely heard a woman's anklets and two people talking softly..."

"Well, it certainly wasn't me!" joked Preeti. "Come, let's get ready. I am sure a good breakfast will improve your mood, Neha. Our waiter told us about the goodies laid out downstairs!"

An hour later, the four youngsters settled down to a hearty breakfast of fluffy omelettes, different breads, French toast, a variety of cheeses and a fruit platter, washed down with steaming cups of freshly brewed coffee.

Rohit knew that Neha was still troubled by the happenings of the previous night. Out of curiosity he asked the old steward, "Tell me, does anyone from the old royal family still live in the fort?"

The steward replied politely, "No Sir. No one. The property belongs to the erstwhile *Maharaja* but the *Raja's* family who lived here were distant cousins. That family is believed to have lived here for generations. They were wealthy, had a lot of land and naturally joined forces to support the ruling *Maharaja* whenever there was an invasion."

"Go on. Tell us more," Rohit coaxed the old man.

The old steward continued, "There is an interesting tale... legend has it... in fact elders in the village, whose ancestors had served the *Raja*, still talk about it, that one of the earlier *Raja's* had four daughters, one, more beautiful than the other. The youngest and the prettiest, also his favourite, was *Rajkumari* Padmavati. One by one, he got his daughters married to wealthy, royal suitors. When it was Padmavati's turn to marry, she refused. The *Raja* found out that Padma had fallen in love with a poor farmer's son from the village. The *Raja* couldn't accept this alliance and seeing his daughter unhappy and pining for her young man, died of grief. His favourite child had broken his heart." The old man had warmed to his subject.

Rohit was very interested. He egged him on. "So what happened to the princess?"

The old man replied, "Well, they say that Padmavati knew that she had broken her father's heart. She decided never to marry. They say she was a good woman and a good queen, kind and loving to her family and subjects. She looked after them and also her father's land. They say her young man from the village also never married. There is also talk that the two lovers met secretly, especially on dark *amavasya* nights. All this must have happened ages ago. Nobody from the *Raja's* family lives here now. We've heard that some descendants have settled in different parts of the country. Some have even gone abroad."

"When is *amavasya*?" asked Rohit.

The old man thought for a moment. "Umm… yesterday. Yes, yesterday was *amavasya*."

Neha jerked her head up when she heard that. 'Was the legend true? It must be. Could it be that she had heard the princess and her lover talking on the ramparts, the night before?' She went cold for a moment. 'Why her? Nobody else had seen or heard this. Or had they?'

Half an hour later the two couples loaded their bags into the car to drive back to Delhi. Neha was relieved to get away. She looked up at the high walls of the fort and said to herself, 'I can understand your anguish Princess, but don't worry. Your secret is safe with me.'

9

NOTA

Mala Rihan

The introduction of a NOTA (None of the above) button on the polling machine has been a longstanding demand of certain activists. They feel that having this button on the polling machine will somehow bring in a major change in Indian politics. When unable to find even one deserving candidate amongst all those listed for the elections, NOTA gives a voter the liberty to cast a vote without selecting one of the undeserving lot. Having read about this, I had decided that in case none of the candidates met my exacting standards, NOTA was the button for me.

Of course, in order to make sure I could use it correctly, I decided to try it out in my daily life. On my next trip to the mall with my wife Anita and my daughters Neha and Meghna, I came across a toy store where the girls rushed in, excited to see the new range of skinny, unattractive Barbie dolls, games etc. A range of five dolls were painstakingly selected by the kids for Dad's final approval. Hoping that as always, he would grandly say, "Take them all," just to see mom frown, at the squandering of all the shopping money on such frivolous purchases.

But not this time! I was determined to use my vote effectively and here was where I would start. Applying NOTA was child's play.

"NOTA!" I said strongly. The sales girl gaped at me. Was I speaking with a forked tongue? Or just some unknown tribal language that I wished to promote?

"NOTA!" was the answer to that as well! I grandly marched out of the store with my unsupportive, most resistant platoon, including one howling girl, in tow.

"NOTA!" was my answer all afternoon to all the choices kept in front of me. I was drunk on the power of NOTA and found it far more exhilarating than opening the wallet to make all these unnecessary purchases. My wife Anita's expressions of dismay, Meghna's tears, Neha's "Pretty please with sugar on it dad!" were all in vain. They did not have the power to move me from my NOTAble position.

Next morning, I woke up happily to the usual sight of the children getting ready and going off to school. Strange, there was no bed tea in sight. "Must have forgotten in the rush," I mumbled, as I got into going-to-work mode. SSS later: Shave, shower and I'm sure you guessed the first ess, I was at the table looking for brekker.

"I'm getting late. Anita, where's my breakfast and tiffin?"

"NOTA!" was the reply.

"Sorry? What was that?" I peered at her over the top of my specs, diverting my attention from my mobile, for just a minute.

"NOTA!" she said, louder and clearer, with a wicked gleam in her eyes.

"What do you mean? I have to go to work. You forgot my bed tea and now you are late with my breakfast…" I trailed off.

"Well you know I looked at all the options for breakfast and tiffin. I thought of cheese omelette and buttered toast with orange juice, *idli sambhar, muttar poha* with *chhas,* and finally thought I'd follow your lead with NOTA! It saves me a lot of time, too. I'm off to college early because I wanted to set up an experiment for the children's biology lab work. See you later..." and off she flew, leaving me gaping at her quick exit.

My "But, but…." was met by a closed door.

Well, that was the end of NOTA for me. I know what the other users of NOTA have yet to find out. NOTA means you're voting for no one and if no one wins how can you?

❏ ❏ ❏

10

The Dust that Wasn't There

Manjula Shukla

"Aw Mom, an arranged marriage in this day and age? You must be out of your mind!" exclaimed Siddhartha.

Renu looked at him affectionately and smiled "*Beta*, you are thirty two now and a practicing surgeon. Isn't it time you settled down?"

"All in good time, Mom" said Sid casually, hiding behind his book "What's the urgency?"

"Well, Kumar Uncle has recommended his friend's daughter very highly. In fact, now it is becoming quite embarrassing. Every time your father speaks with him, he tries to fix a time for a meeting and Papa desperately conjures up reasons to skirt the issue. Let's go and meet the family at least."

"I'm busy. I have to go to the hospital. I have a surgery fixed for noon. You would be interested in this case Mom, it is right up your street..."

"Don't tell lies and don't try to distract me" Renu broke in "I know it's your off today."

"Trust you to catch me out always. Alright, I don't want to."

"You've had enough time to find someone on your own. Now you need to be pushed," said Renu.

"I don't want to be married yet. In fact, I refuse."

"Are you interested in someone, some girl from the medical college, a colleague or some patient's kin, or some friend of a friend?" asked Renu.

"Of course not, Mom, God forbid!"

"Then, what's the harm? Let's go for a few minutes and then politely leave. We can always say that our lifestyles are too different or some innocuous thing so that there are no hard feelings anywhere."

"Mom, let me make it clear, if you exert any pressure I'm going to come back, not home, but to the opposite door and propose to Shrikant uncle's daughter."

Renu and Satish, a silent but highly amused spectator in the mother-son altercation, burst out laughing. Sejal, the neighbour's daughter was all of eighteen and madly in love with Siddhartha for the past fifteen years. One day, Sejal, at the tender age of three, had fallen down the stairs and sprained her ankle. It had been a heartrending sight. She was found sitting at the bottom of the staircase wailing her head off, big eyes drenched with tears behind a mop of untamed curls and Sid, a lanky teenager with a natural aversion for crying kids, nevertheless, carefully picked her up in his arms and deposited her home. Since then, she had been his faithful puppy, worshipping him from afar with her huge eyes.

Last Sunday, the door bell had rung at the ungodly hour of eight o'clock. Surprised, Renu had opened the door to see her on the doorstep with a covered dish in her hand.

"Good morning Aunty, I am sorry to disturb you so early in the morning. I made some *kheer* for Sid, I know he loves it." Siddharta buried himself behind the newspaper and it was left to Renu to make the appropriate noises, thank her profusely and shoo her out. After which, he shoved the newspaper aside and polished off the entire serving with immense glee.

At five in the evening, Satish and Renu with Sid in tow, made their way to the address supplied by Satish's boyhood chum, Ranjit Kumar. It was in the suburbs of the city, a new area being developed. The building was new and well maintained. As they made their way to the fifth floor, Renu cast an appreciative eye around the marble lobby and glass doors. There were many plants placed strategically to create a pleasing decor.

Mr. Mehta opened the door and welcomed them in with a big smile. "Please come in. Ranjit has spoken so much of you all." He ushered them into the drawing room. "Ah, here's Sonali, my daughter. As Ranjit must have told you, my wife passed away some years ago, so now it's just Sonali and me."

An attractive girl in her late twenties entered the room. She was tall, with charming features and wearing a trendy salwar suit. But her eyes had a closed expression and there was an obstinate look on her face. Renu glanced at Sid. His face was set in a ferocious scowl, the one he reserved for scaring the daylights out of junior interns.

Renu's heart sank. This was going to be a tragic affair. The best thing to do would be to leave as soon as possible. She glanced around the room. The cushions were mismatched. The curtains were drawn and the air was heavy. There were no knick-knacks except for some old photographs and portraits from a bygone era, lending their sombreness to the atmosphere. Although the balcony was full of plants there wasn't even a leaf inside. She glanced at Sid. Catching her look, he opened his right hand and straightened his fingers. It was their old signal – 'five minutes'. She signaled back, 'have patience ten minutes at the most.'

"Please sit down. Sonu, get the tea and snacks," said Mr. Mehta. For the sake of social etiquette, they sat down. Sonali came in wheeling a trolley. One look was enough. The cutlets were overdone and the cake looked squishy in the centre.

"It's all homemade" said Mr. Mehta proudly. "Sonali is an excellent cook and housekeeper."

"My foot," thought Renu, mentally looking around for an opportunity to extricate themselves from this impossible situation at the earliest. Her eyes fell on the channel for the sliding window. To her amazement, she saw that it was spotlessly clean. As a housewife, she knew how difficult it was to take the dust out from the grooves. 'Surprising,' she thought and sat up to take a closer look around. The room was squeaky clean. Every nook and cranny was free from dust and cobwebs. There was definitely more to this than met the eye. A nagging suspicion rose in her that perhaps Sonali had deliberately tried to sabotage their first impression of her. Perhaps she, too, had hated being maneuvered into this meeting.

She looked towards Sonali with a warm smile. "Come and sit beside me, Sonali," she said invitingly and patted the chair next to her. She was pleased to see an answering twinkle in her eyes. Perhaps the ice was breaking and the thaw was setting in. "So you are a teacher at St. Maria's convent. Which grades do you teach?" she asked.

"I take junior classes and I teach Maths and English."

"Do you find it interesting?"

"Actually I love it. It's demanding, but very satisfying."

"And what are your hobbies, my dear?"

"Oh, I'm into the usual hobbies reading and music but I love yoga."

"Is it true that doing yoga can prevent any disease?" asked Renu innocently as she herself was a serious practitioner of the art and quite knowledgeable about it.

"Of course, one never needs to go to the doctor if one live according to the principles of yoga," was the unhesitating reply.

"Sid, did you hear this? Sonali says that yoga can prevent any disease. As a doctor, what do you have to say to that?" Renu had set the stage and now she sat back to see the outcome.

Sid rose to the bait and jumped into the arena. "Yoga is fine in its place, but there is no substitute for modern medicine."

"How can you say that? Can medicine cure arthritis or slipped disc?" cut in Sonali sharply.

"What about tumours, can they be cured without medication or surgery?"

"If the person changes his lifestyle and leads a stress free life, even cancer can be cured. There are medically documented cases which prove this." That was just the beginning. Both players in the field circled each other with drawn swords in hand, looking for an opening or a weak spot to plunge in for a fatal thrust.

The elders sat back and enjoyed themselves immensely. Siddhartha, with an unruly lock of hair flopping over one eye, was slicing the air with his hand to emphasize his point. Sonali, with flushed cheeks and sparkling eyes, was counterattacking with dexterity, matching thrust for thrust. Well acquainted with Sid's debating skills, Renu was pleasurably impressed with Sonali's intelligence and communication skills. She was surprised to experience a fervent desire rise from deep within her heart that these two youngsters should explore their compatibility, They seemed to be made for each other.

"Peace, peace," broke in Satish after a while, with an amused smile. "I suggest we continue this discussion tomorrow at our place over dinner. What do you say Mr. Mehta?"

"Of course, it will be a pleasure," Mr. Mehta replied.

"Siddharta and Sonali can think up more arguments to prove their points, right?"

The rest of the evening passed very pleasantly. Once Sid and Sonali had sheathed their swords, they found they had a lot of other common interests to talk about.

Finally it was time to leave. Amid goodbyes, the family took their leave and sat in the car to go home.

"So *beta*, are you off to propose to Sejal?" asked Renu tongue in cheek.

"Aw, Mom," came the answer with a twinkle in the eye "I finally met my match today."

11

Leap of Faith

Rita Chhablani

His mother had ruled the roost. She had been the pint-sized dictator of their home. There had been no doubt about that. She had wielded the rolling pin in the kitchen and out of it too, terror personified.

Children living around a five-mile radius of their home had been petrified of her, for it was she, who tutored them in English. It was because of her that they got perfect scores in their exams. Quietly, without a murmur, they had borne the cane on their knuckles and their ears being twisted mercilessly. If they had dared complain to their mothers, they received a further scolding, instead of receiving a compassionate and patient hearing.

"Ungrateful wretches," they had been screamed at, by their mothers.

Ram, even today, shivered at the thought of his mother. It had not needed much to provoke her. The slightest pretext had been enough to get her into a rage.

With blinders firmly over his eyes, like the horses pulling the tongas in his poor neighbourhood, Ram had trudged to school daily. He had plodded five miles over a bumpy, *kutcha* road with the *mantra* 'must excel, must excel' playing over and over again in his mind with his vision, like that of his favourite mythological hero, Arjuna, focussed on the eye of the bird.

Sometimes, he would stare out of the tiny window of his class room at the clear blue skies and catch sight longingly of a small red kite fluttering in the sky, trying to soar higher, to be one with the birds. He too wanted to be out there, soaring high and far away.

Ram had counted days, praying for his miserable childhood to end. The nights too, did not offer any respite; his tired and perpetually pregnant mother would expect him to clean the mountain of dirty dishes left behind by her fast multiplying brood- there were twelve of his younger siblings already.

His day finally ended after midnight. When the entire household was quiet and asleep, he remembered, he would quietly tip-toe his way to the terrace to keep his date with his beloved *Dadi*. His paternal grandmother would be lying on the stringed cot waiting for him. During this special time with her, she had fed him with stories about mythological heroes who went about charging on white steeds, fighting injustice. It had been his world of escape. He had imagined himself as a knight in shining armour, charging away to different countries, helping people in distress.

His world had revolved around school and the farthest he had ever been was to his *Nani's* home in Chennai.

It was a big city. His grandmother's tiny one-roomed flat had been a treat. From the terrace of the building there had been a good view of Marina beach. There he would stand and glance fixedly at the distant horizon, at the line where the vast expanse of the water seemed to meet the skies. The appearance of an occasional rainbow would gladden his heart. Was there really a pot of gold at the other end, he had often wondered.

And then, would come his mother's sharp strident voice, "Ram, come back," shattering his precious dream world. Gritting his teeth, he would mouth back, "Yes, mummy," and trudge down to his mundane world.

He had hated his mother.

Years passed by. The relief he had felt had been unimaginable, almost indescribable, when he finally left home for the most prestigious engineering college in Bombay.

There it had been a shock for him to experience the hours of arduous study needed, both physical and mental, just to do well in a course. With horror, he had watched the mounting suicides of students unable to bear the pressure of competition. These had been familiar faces, people he had seen on the campus, in class or in the canteen, where everybody had sat poring over books, sharing a friendly cutting *chai*—the Bombay word for splitting the tea by pouring it into the saucer.

Finding himself unable to cope after the first semester, he had said to his parents, "I don't want to be here anymore. I want to come back home." He had been certain, they would understand his cry for help.

Instead, they had screamed the words that were, even today, indelibly etched in his mind. "You ungrateful wretch! We brought you up for this day? Stay there!"

Depressed and miserable, he had returned to his hostel room and had suffered a nervous breakdown soon after. He had warned his friends not to inform his parents. "What is the use?" he had wept to Navin, his close friend. "They will never understand. I want to die."

He had survived and had graduated after four years, but not with flying colours, much to his parents' disappointment. He had not been picked up by any of the blue chip companies that came to the campus for recruitment. After much difficulty he had found placement in a B grade company in Calcutta.

He had left for the new city, where he knew not a soul, and had rented a room close to his place of work in Chowringhee. He had found solace in work and would often return home late at night on a cycle rickshaw, pulled by one of the scrawny Bihari drivers, who would sing along merrily as they made their way through the narrow by lanes. The songs had always been so joyful and soothing. There had been acceptance and joy in them. He had often wondered.

And then, he had started watching them. The stand had been located on the street below his room. Switching off the light, he would stand by the window and peer into their world, seeing them happily eat their modest meal of *satu*, pounded, roasted chickpeas. How could they be happy with so little? He had made a decision to explore their lives.

Soon, in his free hours, he was following them around. One day he was led right to the door step of a toothless old man, who seemed to be their *Guru*.

Ram had sat down before him. He had listened, transfixed, to his words. Finally, he had understood the secret of how these simple poor folks could have this joie de vivre pouring out of them, of how they could accept their tough life with a smile.

He had fallen at the feet of the old man. "*Baba*, please accept me, I need peace," he had wept.

Within a short time, he had become his most fervent disciple. Ram had finally understood life. His turbulent mind had settled down after all these years in his search for that elusive peace and found the balance that he had been denied so far.

The next three years had been the best he had experienced in his life. And then his parents had woken up and announced that it was time their eldest son be tied down in holy matrimony and settle down in life. An eligible bachelor like their son, Ram was not safe in a new and strange city so far away from home. They got into action and had contacted all their relatives in Ahmedabad. They in turn had reached out to various matchmakers. They soon began spreading the word about Ram and his glowing achievements: an IITian, tall, fair and handsome, hailing from an honourable lineage, and looking for a match of equal standing.

Hundreds of photographs had begun pouring in. His parents, delirious with joy, had hastened to Ahmedabad, After careful sifting they had picked one. The girl was a rare combination of great beauty and domesticity, noble virtues and a lineage that was higher than theirs. And the icing on the cake, she was rich too!

All this activity had been going on clandestinely, without Ram's knowledge. One day, his father's letter had arrived asking him to come to Ahmedabad on such-and-such a date. Indoctrinated to be an obedient son, he had at once procured a train ticket and set forth for the long journey to the mill city, situated on the opposite coast from Calcutta.

Even then, he had been blissfully ignorant. How could one have been so naive? This thought kept pricking his mind and he tried to push it away. He scolded himself for still being so vulnerable.

But the deluge of old memories did not discontinue and poured forth with vengeful force.

As soon as he had reached, his father had asked him to freshen up, even selected the shirt he should wear. As soon as he was ready, his parents had asked him to accompany them along with some distant relatives, who he had later discovered had been the fellow perpetrators of the crime, to some strange bungalow in a posh locality known as Navrangpura.

He had watched his parents looking around with awe at the huge, chandeliered drawing room, the size of a hotel's banquet hall. For some strange reason he had felt as though they were sizing up the place, as though they were going to buy it.

Why were they here, he had wondered and whom were they visiting. His mind had been exploding with a thousand questions but he had kept his mouth shut.

Used to stainless steel utensils at home, soon, they were being served Darjeeling tea in fine bone china cups. He had found it very discourteous when he saw his parents and relatives gobbling down the melt-in-the-mouth, generously buttered chutney sandwiches, and wolfing down the array of cakes, pastries and *pakodas*.

"Excellent, excellent," his awed mother had kept repeating.

"So, I consider the match fixed," the bride's *paan*-chewing, rotund father had announced matter-of-factly, as though he had been reading today's weather report.

Ram had been so absorbed in watching with distaste, the obese man's lips stained an ugly orange by the betel leaf, that he failed to hear the significant words.

Neither did he hear his parents parroting the line, "The match is fixed, fixed."

The horrible man had sprung up from the sofa and to Ram's horror, enveloped him in a big hug. Ram had recoiled as though a scorpion had stung him. It was then that the realization had dawned on him, that they had been talking about his marriage and he was the *bali ka bakra*. Truly, the lamb to the slaughter!

One look at the chiffon clad, manicured, pencil-thin eye-browed wife-to-be who had been sitting quietly on one of the sofas and Ram had wanted to burst out, "They are not our type! I will not marry her!"

He had stared at his parents for help.

But they had been busy hugging each other and their mouths were being stuffed with sweets, without even a second glance at him.

At home, he had tried to mumble his objections, "Beneath the opulence is an utter lack of culture," and so on, but his dominating parents had overruled each one of them.

***

A month later...

He had been wed, standing like a joker on the stage in a posh hotel in Ahmedabad where everyone but him, seemed to be enjoying themselves. He had felt he was in a cruel nightmare from which he was soon going to wake up. When he did not, his feet had wanted to take flight as soon as he sat with his new bride in the flower bedecked, bridal Mercedes. His old *karma* had come home to roost and he'd better suffer it or accept it, he had heard his Guru's words echo in his ears.

Suffer it, he knew. But accept it? He did not know for how long. Tears ran down his eyes.

***

"*Jai ho Maharajki,*" reverberated voices, wave like, through the vast grounds of the NSCI club of Bombay.

"Obeisance to our Guru," chimed the foreign devotees, trancelike, flinging their arms up in the sky.

With a start, the eyelids of the one now known as the 'Knower of the Supreme Knowledge,' fluttered open. A beatific smile on his face, Swami Parmananda looked around with twinkling eyes at the ocean of people. Some disciples said the eyes were hypnotic, while others felt compassion streamed out of them. He had been declared the 'Guru of the Century.'

After a whirlwind tour of villages, the guru had just reached the metropolis of Bombay. It was the sheer magic of his words, the genuineness, the care behind them that drew people from all over the world around him, like bees to honey. When he had been selected as the successor on his Guru's departure to the Himalayas, he had arrived at once. Then on, all he had wanted to do was spread his Master's teachings and walk firm in his footsteps.

Soundless, the masses sat listening. Not even a leaf fluttered. "My dear children, it is all destiny and our *karma* that create what we suffer or enjoy. Our relationships are nothing but the give-take, the *lena-dena*, the balances to be settled with different people from our past lives. They leave when your account with them is settled. The only true relationship is with the Lord. Become a Meerabai, a Radha... saints such as these," he said, looking around, his eyes meeting each person's in the audience.

Suddenly, he stopped at a pair of eyes that were staring fixedly at him, a glimmer of recognition in them, tears pouring unabashedly down this old woman's cheeks.

A shudder ran down his spine, accompanied by a flash of recognition. It was his mother!

He, the Swamiji now, had been Ram in another lifetime. Images of the past went by in rapid succession. After a year of his marriage, and before the children could arrive, unable to take it anymore, he remembered that he had grimly walked out of the door of his flat one day and vanished as though from the face of the earth.

He had been conscious of all the missing person advertisements his parents had placed in the newspapers, begging him to return, offering desperate rewards when he did not respond. Another year passed by with no news of him. After exhaustive rounds of all the hospitals and police stations, his family had given up hope.

After some time, he had seen his picture in the newspaper once again, with an announcement about his death, and a ceremony being organised in the local temple.

He had given a sigh of relief. The story of a boy called Ram, was over. He must be a picture on the wall in his parents' home by now. He was free and had achieved *moksha* from his earthly bondages.

Ram, aka Swami Parmananda, shut his eyes to switch off such unwanted musings. His past was dead. He did not want to be pulled by the strings of relationships, even his mother's. He had forgiven them, cut all attachments asunder and thrown them to burn in the fire, along with his old clothes. He had donned a monk's robe on the banks of the holy river Ganga and taken on the role of the new *Guru* of the ashram.

He turned his face away from the sad eyes and quickly got up. The devotees burst into tumultuous, "*Jai ho, jai ho*," when they saw him getting off the dais and slipping his feet into the wooden *khadau*, his new footwear after he had joined the order.

Wanting to make a getaway, he quickly walked through the human passage created by the organisers to keep the thronging crowds at bay, and to his humble car, the Ambassador. Not for him the Rolls Royce his hosts had sent for the dinner tonight. He was firm about his principles.

He was about to step into his car when he heard that familiar voice from childhood say, "*Beta*." Son! His mother's glance was searching his eyes for an answer, for an affirmation. He knew she had recognised him.

"Driver, go," he barked brusquely, startling the man in the front seat into action. The car started moving away. At once, he felt contrite at his rude behaviour, so he turned around and waved at her. He saw the tears running down her cheeks but turned away and shut his eyes.

It was only when they had reached their destination, that he let out a sigh of relief. After 15 years, he was still vulnerable! He settled down on the ostentatious sofa in the living room of his host's home. More austerities and *sadhana*, prayers and introspection were needed. He knew he was lacking and had to be careful, as he sat listening to melodious devotional songs.

After the question and answer session, he was respectfully taken to the dining table. He was surprised when his host vanished as soon as the prayer of gratitude was done. He was about to place a morsel of the bitter gourd *bhaji* into his mouth, when the elderly man reappeared.

Bending humbly by Ram's side he begged, *"Guruji*, I would like you to bless my son and daughter-in-law," clearing the way for a balding man and a middle aged woman who had been standing behind him.

Swami Parmananda, (Ram) nodded and looked up, straight into the eyes of his ex-wife. Second time around, she had done well for herself, marrying into this affluence. He pitied the poor husband, for despite his riches, there was no happiness on the man's face. In fact, he seemed pretty miserable. God bless him, give him peace!

***

A village near Chennai

That night, as Ram lay on his bed in the sparsely furnished room in his ashram, his last thought before he shut his eyes, was that life was truly a cycle. What you run away from follows you and stares at you right in the face, and deal with it you must.

He sat up. Soon, he slipped into a state of deep meditation.

When he opened his eyes, it was the early hours of dawn. With it came the realization, that the last lesson life had brought his way, all these people from the past, had been for a purpose.

Now on, nothing would rattle him any more.

He was finally Swami Parmananda in the true sense! His *Guru*, now very old and living in the Himalayas in some cave, would be proud of him.

It was time to go and meet him!

❏ ❏ ❏

12

Bus to Bhuleshwar

Shenaz A. Setna

Heads turned and eyes squinted in the sun as the red, double-decker BEST bus lumbered down the road towards the bus–stop. Anxious faces peered at the number written in the display window. Was it the one they wanted? "Number 126!" a man shouted out in a raspy voice, amidst the din and roar of the constant stream of traffic, followed by a shrill female voice, "That's ours, girls!"

The crowd surged forward and the usual confusion prevailed. Passengers tried to alight, as others pushed their way in determinedly. Most of the passengers belonged to the working class, conspicuous amongst them and in total contrast, were four college girls. They were alternatively giggling away and grumbling about the men on the bus, who were up to their usual surreptitious pinching and harassment. Their fresh young faces, energy and zest for life made even the dour and jaded bus-conductor smile for a few seconds.

The 4 young girls had bunked their college classes and were embarking on a shopping trip. The festive season was around the corner, and they were awaiting the results of their half-yearly exams. People were more in a mood to celebrate than the last year, which had been dominated by the State of Emergency imposed by the Prime Minister, Mrs. Indira Gandhi. However, they were as usual, on a tight budget, with a long gift list of family and friends.

Tina, a classmate, who had been desperately trying to befriend the other three girls over the last few months had suggested this trip by the bus number 126 to Bhuleshwar, where, she insisted, everything they wanted would be available at a much lower price than the high street. Her entire family shopped there themselves. Zara, a tiny slip of a girl, with flashing dark eyes and a temper to match was the only other girl who had actually been to Bhuleshwar, albeit in her childhood years, and had no recollection of it at all. She normally hated going to crowded, noisy places, but was game to go there with her friends.

The bus crawled its way through the dense traffic as the girls inched their way down the aisle, hoping for a little space to stand in a little comfort. The conductor was busy at the entry point, controlling the crowd and issuing tickets. He did not venture into the seating area for quite some time.

"Look after your bags, girls, be careful!" exclaimed Ayesha, after she felt her bag strap being tugged at a couple of times. She was the mother-hen of the trio, who were very close friends from their school days. She was quiet and reserved but looked out for the other two, especially Zara, and rescued them quite often from their escapades. She was extremely generous and kind and the other two looked after her by preventing her generosity from being taken advantage of, and provided a lively and comic relief to her otherwise isolated and lonely life. The trio had been nicknamed by a college classmate as "The Mad Hatter, The March Hare and The Dormouse" after the characters in Alice in Wonderland.

"Yes Grandma!" exclaimed Nina, "The March Hare." She was born in March, was tall and lanky, absent minded and always rushing about in a hurry. As she turned to reply to Ayesha, she noticed that Tina, who had climbed up into the bus behind them, was not to be seen. "She must be around in this crowd somewhere, we will look for her later," she thought to herself.

By this time, the conductor had reached the girls. "*Chaar* ticket, Bhuleshwar" said Ayesha holding out the money. "*Nahi, teen,*"[1] shot back Nina, "That Tina can get her own ticket, as she's never around, when it's time to pay!"

"*Par ye* bus Bhuleshwar *nahi jaati,*" said the conductor, to which the girls dropped their jaws in horror and disbelief.

"*To kaha jaati hai?*"[2] asked a bewildered Zara. The conductor stared at the three girls' questioning and yet innocent faces and felt a twinge of conscience, compassion and concern. He hated this route, but after several months had become slightly more impervious to the dirt, stench and sleaze emanating from both the place and people around him. "*Tumko khabar nahi? Ye bus Jijamata Udyaan tak normally jaati hai. Abhi ye bus to aadhe rasta se vaapas Mantralaya jayeegi! Parantu Bhuleshwar se nahi!*"[3]

"*Kaha se?*"[4] snarled Zara, advancing a couple of steps towards him, bewilderment giving way to anger. Ayesha immediately put a restraining hand on Zara's shoulder.

"*Achha area nahi, red light area hai!*"[5] the conductor said in a voice just above a whisper.

"Oh my God!" screeched Nina. Ayesha's mouth opened and closed like a goldfish, and her normal calmness and composure gave way to a bit of annoyance and anxiety.

---

1 No, three   2 Then where does it go?

3 You don't know? This bus normally goes to Jijamata Udyaan. Now it will return via Mantralaya. But not through Bhuleshwar.   4 From where?

5 Not a nice area, it is a red light area.

"Where on earth is that blasted Tina?" she said in a very low, terse and abrupt tone. As all three girls craned their necks and twisted their heads around to look for her, they noticed, that not only had the number of passengers decreased; but there were hardly any women left in the bus, there was one old crone sitting near the exit and a couple of garishly dressed young women with provocatively draped sarees and cholis and layers of make-up applied with a heavy hand. The type of men on board had changed too, most of them openly ogling them and passing lewd comments, accompanied by laviscious winks, smiles and gestures. Tina however, was nowhere to be seen.

"Tina told me that the last stop would be at the Bhuleshwar market area," exclaimed Zara heatedly.

"What do we do now?" asked a very pale and quiet Ayesha. She was scared now, but only a slight wobble in her voice betrayed her anxiety and fear. She looked quite calm and her face had her customary quiet steady expression.

"Ab kya kare?"[6] demanded Nina of the bus conductor. By this time, the bus was firmly ensconced in a huge unmoving mass of vehicles, vendors and pedestrians, none of whom would give right of way to the other, thus preventing any further movement. The conductor peered through the glass window pane and then turned back to the girls. *"Yaha utar jao! Kissi ko puch ke vaapas jaana."*[7]

The girls alighted from the bus in a daze and nearly got knocked down by the pressing crowd of people, handcarts and vendors all vying for position and space.

"Hold hands girls!" cried out Zara, eyes flashing in temper and a scowl on her pretty face. She had had a brief look at Ayesha's pale tense face and decided to take action. "We'll go over to the side and ask the *paanwalla* for directions."

---

6 Ab kya Kare - What is to be done now?
7 Yaha uter jao - get off Ask someone about how to return

As the girls approached the *paanwalla's* stall, a couple of seedy looking youths with greasy lanky hair, gaudy coloured shirts with buttons partly undone, half smoked cigarettes hanging from their lips, sidled up to them.

"What you want baby? Rocky get for you. Best quality and best price!" said the taller of the two in a harsh guttural voice.

The girls were petrified. It was obvious even to them that the young man was referring to drugs. Even the quick-thinking, quick witted, street-smart Zara was stumped for words. They huddled up into one another for support and protection looking around them in vain, for a quick and safe exit route from their current dilemma. And when they heard the next few words they nearly jumped out of their skins with shock and fright.

"What are you three girls doing over here? Have you taken leave of your senses? Do you know where you are and what type of area this is? You look like you have come from decent families. Tell me now!"

As the three girls swung around to face the man who had bellowed out these questions, their faces frozen in expressions of terror and panic, the two youths slipped away. As they looked up slowly, their faces became unfrozen and they sighed with relief in unison. Standing in front of them was a big, burly police inspector with two policemen in tow.

Zara stood on tiptoe to see him better, and with a great effort, kept her voice steady as she asked him, "Can you help us sir? We wanted to go to Bhuleshwar to do some shopping, but we landed up here by mistake. The bus got stuck in a traffic jam and the conductor told us it would be better to get off here!"

One of the policemen looked skeptical; he had seen too many pretty young things indulging in not very pretty things, often with disastrous consequences. He informed the inspector in a quiet tone that Bhuleshwar was not anywhere in the vicinity.

Nina overheard him and cried out, "But we didn't know that! We've never been to Bhuleshwar before! Tina told us to take the 126 bus as it would be cheaper than sharing a taxi."

"Which one of you is Tina?" asked the inspector.

"None of us, sir." said Ayesha quietly, finally finding her voice. "She disappeared while we were on the bus. We don't know where or when she got out."

"Or why?" exclaimed the inspector and Zara together and exchanged a brief glance and smile. *"Chalo,* come with me and we'll get you out of here quickly before you get into any more trouble. Follow me, and don't stop or look at anything or anybody. My men are behind you. Don't worry." He marched forward into the crowd, swinging his baton to make way through the succession of narrow lanes, until they reached the police jeep parked on the side of a main road. The inspector ushered them into the back of the jeep and went in front to talk to the driver and his companion. He came back with a small piece of paper. "I have written down my name and the number of the police station where I am currently posted. My men will escort you back to VT. Next time please be more careful. And yes, just one question, who is this Tina?"

"A college friend sir," said Nina.

"I would advise you to stay away from her, she's trouble." he replied, after which he waved his hand, and with the radio crackling away and beacon flashing, the jeep soon wound its way into town and deposited the girls outside VT station. The girls thanked the policemen sincerely.

"Sambhal ke ghar jaana. Yeh time bach gaye,"[8] warned the driver sternly, before he steered his jeep into the teeming traffic again.

---

8 Take care was return home. You were safe this time.

They looked at each other and simultaneously lifted their arms to hail a taxi. The give lived quite close to each other and reached their homes, safe and sound. The tale of their escapade was related to their families and the next day to all their college classmates. They enjoyed being the centre of attention for a few days. Tina however, was conspicuously absent and all calls to her residence went unanswered.

A fortnight passed before Tina finally showed up in college. She was immediately pounced upon by Ayesha, Nina and Zara and an explanation demanded.

"I'm sorry I left you on the bus like that! My family was going through a difficult patch due to my father's business problems, so I replied to an advertisement for an escort agency. However, the type of clients worsened and I wanted to leave, but needed the money. I was told that I could earn some extra money if I introduced more girls to the agency. My boss was going to pick you up at the last bus-stop..." With her head hung she whispered, "But I got scared and got off the bus. Sorry!" She burst into tears. "Please don't tell anyone else. My parents found out and were very angry with me. Please forgive me."

Soft-hearted Ayesha's heart melted and she put an arm around the sobbing girl to console her. Zara glared at her in anger, but surprisingly it was the scatter-brained Nina who had the last word. She calmly removed Ayesha's arm from Tina's shoulder. "You put us into a very dangerous situation because of your deviousness and thoughtlessness. Forgive you? It will take us all some time to do that, if we ever do."

Then she turned towards her friends, smiled and said, "Come on you two. Our classes are over and we've got shopping to do!"

"On one condition," piped up the normally quiet Ayesha, "...we are going to Colaba and Breach Candy! I never want to go anywhere near Bhuleshwar or on the 126 number bus in my life again!" Her friends nodded their heads in agreement as they swung out of the college gates, grins of anticipation writ large on their faces.

As they say, "Retail therapy is the best therapy!"

❑ ❑ ❑

13

Spoilt for Choice

Jayashree Dhillon

Mrs Singh was in the shower, with water running down her head and into her eyes. After a few minutes of enjoying the warm spray on her back, she started looking for the bath soap. She looked around the bathroom. Cabinets, shelves and window sills were full of bottles and containers in every size, shape and colour. Where was the soap?

Mrs Singh was short-sighted. So without her glasses, she had to pick up every bottle, bring it close to her eyes, squint at the label to see if there was anything she could use, instead of the missing soap.

Mrs Singh was in an unfamiliar bathroom. She was in Bangalore to attend a teachers' training workshop. Her dear friend and colleague, Mrs Suman Sharma, in Chandigarh, had insisted that Mrs Singh stay with her daughter Shikha, who worked in Bangalore, instead of in a hotel. Suman Sharma had exclaimed, "My daughter Shikha is a friendly, young girl. She lives alone, so she would love some company. You must stay with her. I'll phone her right away. She'll be happy to have you at her place."

Shikha was a bubbly person, warm and caring. She had made Mrs Singh most comfortable. She had picked up Mrs Singh from the airport and taken her home to her small and pretty flat. She had laid out a sumptuous tea with sandwiches, carrot cake and banana chips. After a leisurely tea, Shikha had led Mrs Singh to her neat room. There were fresh flowers in a crystal vase and the latest magazines on a bed side table. "I have kept a fresh towel for you in the bathroom, Aunty and also a new cake of soap," added Shikha.

Now where was that soap?

Mrs Singh picked up a bottle of body wash. She had never liked the idea of using a viscous, thick liquid, so luxuriously called a shower-gel, for her bath. She preferred the good, old fashioned soap and water routine. Mrs Singh decided to go through some more bottles. She went through a couple of them. They turned out to be shampoos. 'Hair-Fall Control'; 'Total Damage Control'; 'Damage Repair Plus'; 'Strong and Shiny'; each label announced grandly—as if to say, "Pick me up. I am the best!" Many international brands were part of that collection.

Next to the shampoos, there were several bottles of conditioners. Mrs Singh had never used a hair-conditioner before. Her two daughters had often chided her in the past, 'You must condition your hair, Ma. You'll see the difference in your hair at once. How can you not use a conditioner?' Mrs Singh had never had any patience to spend time in such frivolous pursuits. 'Imagine,' she thought to herself, 'first shampoo one's hair, then rub conditioner 'from roots to the tips' of your hair, wait for a minute and then wash it all off, till the water runs clear!' She couldn't be bothered about these things. She read some more labels: 'for bounce and beauty'; 'for tangle-free hair'; 'for manageable and lustrous locks'—very enticing but she couldn't have had a bath with a conditioner!

Her eyes moved over to two colourful tins, each printed with lovely bunches of flowers. One label read, 'Blossoms' and the other, 'Blooming Buds.' She picked up one tin. It smelt heavenly. She peered at the tin, it was talcum powder! She couldn't possibly use that for soap!

Mrs Singh squinted at some more labels. She read, 'Soft as Silk'; 'Pearly Glow'; 'Fresh and Clean'; 'Satin Finish' on bottles with pictures of pretty girls or clusters of peaches, pomegranates and cherries. Luscious fruit that looked good enough to eat! That was an arrangement of lotions and potions for the skin. They were face washes. Mrs. Singh, finally, settled for a face wash, 'Clean and Soft', from an international brand and completed her bath.

After indulging in this luxury of a bath and body collection, Mrs. Singh got tempted to go through the shelf adorned with skin creams and moisturisers. There again, she was spoilt for choice—'Peaches & Cream'; 'Soft Touch' and 'Cream & Honey'. Then there were some jars of body butter. Butter? Ugh! The idea of slathering butter on one's body–instead of toast–was not very appealing. But the jars were so pretty and in such lovely colours, she couldn't help taking a closer look. There was variety there too. Each body butter came with its own exciting fruit fragrance: 'Vanilla Bliss'; 'Cranberry Crush' and 'Mango Tango'. She picked up the safest one. How bad can vanilla be? But ended up smelling like an ice cream!

Emerging from the bathroom, she said to Shikha, "Where did you keep the soap, Shikha? I couldn't find it and had to have a bath with your expensive face wash!"

Totally unfazed, Shikha replied, "That's okay Aunty, but the soap is there, I got it only for you. I don't use soap!"

There it was, the missing soap, hidden behind the array of bottles.

"Nobody uses soap anymore Aunty, even you shouldn't. It's not good for your skin."

Mrs Singh picked up the soap and smiled to herself. The wrapper said it all, "Get rid of fine lines and wrinkles. For mature skin. With added moisturisers!"

14

Doon Days

Mala Rihan

The air was crisp, cold and clear. A slight shower during the night had rendered in glistening black, the branches of the cherry blossom tree in the garden. A sprinkling of white on the twigs was an indicator of beauty and flowering yet to come.

It had been a quiet, fairly normal winter session at the school, it was enlivened only by the squabbling of the girls, the occasional bout of high spirits that the dull winter could not suppress for long. Then there were the gossipy tidbits about the last time someone from the nearby boys school had tried to scale the walls in an attempt to see his latest heart throb.

And now I was holding my breath, wondering when the storm would break and carry us all away in its fury.

***

It all began innocuously enough, with me wandering into the room of my fellow teacher Ayesha to ask for a red pen to complete my corrections. It was late in the evening and I was rather casually dressed in pajamas and a pair of oversized cozy slippers. I pushed open the door but, to my surprise, it did not yield. I gave the three knocks that identified a friend, and Ayesha opened the door with a finger on her lips to procure my silence. As I stepped in, I realized that there was someone in the room, in fact a rather large someone who was sitting in the only chair, looking a little sheepish. He was very dark, handsome in a rather rugged way.

"Danny is very ill and Sameer has come to tell me that he has to be hospitalized immediately," said Ayesha. This accounted for the presence of a male in an all ladies hostel at this late hour. Ayesha had confided in me that she was very fond of Sameer, but they were going through a difficult phase in their relationship. However I hadn't met him before this.

Danny was a young upcoming crooner whom I had briefly met at a barbeque recently. He was young, good looking. That evening, he had strummed the guitar as he sang, "Suzanne takes you down to a place by the river..." in his soft, deep voice.

"How sad. What's wrong with him?" I asked.

"He has had an asthmatic attack," said Sameer as he rose from his chair. "I must leave now."

And he was out of the back door with a quick stride. It was dark outside. For such a large man he moved very silently, his feet barely crunching the gravel as he reached the gate. After a slight delay, we heard his bike start in the distance. It was then that Ayesha continued the story about Danny. She was still quite agitated but I put it down to the bad news and spent a while chatting before going back to my room. 'Oh no. I have forgotten the pen. I'll have to work through recess to finish,' I mumbled to myself as I settled into bed.

The following Saturday afternoon, Sameer was visiting again. Ayesha called me in to meet him.

"How's Danny now?" I asked.

"Oh he's ok. He's off to Delhi for a concert," replied Sameer.

"Huh? Wasn't he at death's door?" I thought, but put it aside as I went in to my room. After a while there was a knock on my door. To my surprise it was Sameer standing there with Ayesha watching him like a hawk from the door of her room.

"Go on. Ask her," she prompted. Sameer seemed to turn a deeper shade of red under his tan. He seemed rather annoyed and I assumed this was one more of their tiffs.

"Would you come with me to the club for drinks and dinner tonight?" asked Sameer.

I couldn't believe my ears. Whatever had got into the guy?

"I've told him I'm not going. Why don't you go?" added Ayesha snappily. Obviously there was no sense in being a part of this quarrel, I thought and began a polite refusal.

"There! Didn't I tell you no one will go out with someone as uncouth as you," she taunted.

Sameer was tall, but years spent on the farm doing heavy work which had darkened his skin and roughened his hands. He was a farmer and looked it. But he was well bred, very handsome if a trifle swarthy, and was also very charming.

I made a snap decision. "Sure I'll come"

Smiling, Sameer said that he'd pick me up at seven.

Well, it was time to dress up. Out came my mother's emerald green chiffon sari with the beautiful brocade blouse. And the heels, which I hadn't even unpacked since coming from Bombay. Quite a change from the cotton sarees and *khadi kurtas* that I usually sported. Not bad, I thought as I looked at the mirror, spraying a bit of Chanel 5 for extra effect.

Sameer was at my door punctually, dressed very smartly with tie and jacket and leather shoes instead of his usual sturdy boots.

"Wow! You look gorgeous," he said loudly, as he escorted me to the bike. As we looked at each other, we giggled shyly at our newfound friendship, and our attempt to get Ayesha to come around. She had a forced, tight smile on her lips as she waved goodbye.

To our mutual surprise, we had a great evening together, chatting away like old friends once the ice had been broken. Though I'd only met him a few times, his relationship with my fellow teacher provided enough of an ice breaker. He confided that he was keen to marry her but she had been leading him a merry dance, and had not shown too much interest. He did not know if she was playing hard to get or whether she felt her parents would not approve of this match.

The wine was excellent and we made a meal of Chinese food at the club dining room. A vast domed structure; it had many relics of the British era still adorning its walls. We wandered around with our coffee, examining artifacts and paintings on the walls. When we finally returned, we found the gates to my cottage closed. Only then did we realize that we had overshot the 10:30 pm deadline.

"Not a problem," said Sameer, taking in my shocked look. Before I could get a word out he had stood me on the bike, and effortlessly helped me across the gate. Our goodnights were subdued so as not to arouse the senior teacher Mrs. P. who lived in the same bungalow.

***

"Madam?" Anita's shrill voice penetrated into my pleasant reverie.

"Yes, my dear?"

"Ma'am, I can't do the last problem." "Yes Ma'am!" chorused the voices from behind her.

I switched effortlessly to the role of smart, efficient, schoolteacher. Looking at the Maths problem, I saw instantly what they had failed to grasp. "Okay, let's try it on the board.

Shefali, would you like to come up and solve it?"

The kids loved this little break from their routine. A little smiling interaction and a few jokes brought the sunshine into the room—always welcome on a chilly winter morn. The bell rang just as we finished. I collected my books and walked straight into Mamta and Rajul, two of the most nosy and gossipy middle school teachers 'Oh God! How was I to escape?' On a happy thought, I slid back into class and said, "The rest of the sums on Page 95 are very simple. Do them for homework and I'll see you tomorrow!"

I could see the teachers' backs as they went past me to their classrooms, and mentally patted myself on the back for my quick thinking. There was hope for me yet!

Mid-morning, during my free time, I took a chair and table in the garden outside the staffroom and sat pensively chewing on a pencil. The pile of books stayed as it was while I frowned at the one in my hand. What happy days we'd had!

Thoughts of a picnic to Bear valley came to color my day. It was on a bright and warm Sunday that we had elected to escape from our humdrum routine and go off for a picnic. Sameer, Vijay, Sandeep and Manisha had joined Ayesha and me. We had diverted from our usual course and the three mobikes smoothly took the new, rather untrodden, path. Sitting behind Vijay, I watched Ayesha and Sameer do daredevil stunts on their bike. She was standing on the back, long straight hair streaming out behind her.

"Oh! What a lovely waterfall! Let's stop right here," exclaimed Ayesha. We were all enchanted by the beautiful, natural grove. Pine trees guarded it on all sides and the gushing waters of a natural spring came down in a magnificent waterfall, into a deep shaded pool.

"This looks like the place for our picnic." said Sameer enthusiastically.

"Are you sure?" demurred Vijay, "It is a lonely place and may not be too safe." There had been cases of robbery and the boys liked to play it safe when they had girls around. In fact one of them was even carrying a gun,

'It'll be ok! Don't worry so much. After all we're three and the girls are in fine fettle too," threw in Sandeep, clinching the argument.

So we put down our colorful *durries*, our purses and the picnic lunches that the boys had got from their homes. Sandeep and Vijay stayed with their parents and the moms were happy to provide a lavish spread in true north Indian style for us.

"Wow! *Aloo parathas…* don't mind but I'm going to start." said Manisha. I could still taste the fab *rossagullas* that Sandeep had brought.

***

"Where do you think she's gone?" It was Manisha's worried question that brought me back to the present. "Hi! Didn't see you coming." I dodged the direct question.

"Yes, I could see you were busy with corrections! "said Manisha sarcastically. "So where is she?"

"Your guess is as good as mine," I parried, unwilling to state my fears out loud.

Ayesha had not been seen since Friday evening. I had last seen her at tea at 4 pm. It was now Tuesday morning and she was still missing. We were none the wiser about her whereabouts. But there was a ghastly suspicion that she might have gone to Sameer's village.

Sameer and Ayesha's relationship had been tempestuous from the start. Days of fun and happiness were followed by bitter words and fights, with alarming regularity.

Was it only ten days ago that Sameer had abruptly announced that his parents had chosen a bride for him and that he was to be married shortly? It was a Saturday afternoon and we were having tea at one of our favorite haunts—a tea stall on the famous Raipur road. Sitting on string cots at a place more frequented by truck drivers, we were watching the sunset when this announcement came out of the blue.

Ayesha's face darkened and she lashed out at Sameer both verbally and physically. Luckily, it was only Manisha and me watching. Slapping him on the right cheek, she started a tirade of foul language that I hesitate to put down here.

Sameer looked at her, and I could see no love on his face— just resignation and pity. He stood up, picked up the tab, paid, and kicked his bike to a start in utter silence. In a minute he was gone. Manisha and I looked at each other, horrified at this sudden turn of events. Our sympathies were divided—Sameer was a great guy and Ayesha had been giving him a hard time, but this way of breaking the news was horrible. No matter how tough she pretended to be, Ayesha was just a 24 year-old-girl, and she was very deeply involved with this guy. We consoled her as best as we could and returned, packed all together on Manisha's scooter.

The next few days Ayesha had been very closed and quiet. She was unwilling to discuss what had happened and also made it clear that she neither looked for nor wanted any sympathy. Thinking that she was sulking, we had kept our distance and respected her wish to be alone.

"What can we do? Supposing the principal asks us where she is." The words burst out of me. Manisha was the only one I could confide in.

In a hushed whisper she answered, "We'll say we don't know. That is the truth. It is the principal's business to control and keep track of her teachers. Stop Worrying."

"Do you think she's gone after him? She couldn't have been so foolish!"

The lunch bell put an end to our discussion.

"Where's Ayesha? Her class was making such a racket I couldn't hear myself sing. I had to go and fire them. Is she ill?" This was directed at me by the music teacher Ms. Gadgil.

"No I don't think so. But I haven't seen her. I came in a hurry." It sounded lame to my ears but was accepted and we moved on to our classes.

In the evening, sitting on my terrace, Manisha and I continued our musings. "I'll have to report her absence." It was already four days since I had seen her last.

"Why didn't he want to marry Ayesha?" Manisha enquired.

"I don't think he ever asked her. Probably found it difficult because she spoke so vehemently against the institution of marriage. She was a woman's libber and wanted a live-in relationship." 'Marriage destroys love. And for a woman it also destroys her entire career and life.' These defiant words summed up Ayesha's attitude. No wonder Sameer had not proposed to her!

Early next morning there was a knock at my window. "Open the door. It's me."

"Ayesha!" I leapt out of my cozy bed heedless of the chill winter air. Running to the side door, I threw it open. A bedraggled Ayesha appeared, only to be dragged in unceremoniously by me. What a sight she was! Face puffed, hair tangled, and clothes–I think she'd been wearing those since the day she left!

Throwing open my door, I ushered her into my room, put a blanket around her quivering shoulders and handed her a tissue as she sneezed loudly.

"What happened? Where were you?" I couldn't stop myself from asking. I gathered my wits together and said, "Wait a minute. I'll make you some tea."

As she sipped the sweet hot tea gratefully, the story tumbled out.

"He was getting married. Why couldn't he ask me? I went there to his father's house in Kanatal. They were getting engaged. He was looking so handsome in his *achkan* and *mojris*. He pretended not to know me. I tried to talk to him but his sister wouldn't let me, she drew me out of there so fast, and put me in a car with instructions to the driver to drop me at the station. His father had such a forbidding demeanor. I wish… I wanted… I thought he loved me! But…" Incoherent bits of story popped out as she tried to make sense of what had happened.

My heart went out to her. Giving her a hug, I told her she deserved someone better.

"I have to go but don't you stir. I'll tell the Principal that you have the flu. Stay in bed for today. I'll send Pappu with breakfast for you." I told her as I left for school.

The cherry blossom tree was black and bare once more. The white flowers heralding spring had fallen off overnight. The ground was wet. Had there been a storm?

❏ ❏ ❏

15

Debts from Past Life

Manjula Shukla

The air conditioned bus ran smoothly on the expressway, on its way from Pune to Mumbai. It was Sunday evening and the bus was full. Weekly commuters, living in one city and working in another, made this trip regularly, refreshed after a leisurely weekend, recharged and ready to face the hectic week ahead.

In the front row was a young couple. They looked as if they were professionals in the field of Information Technology. The wife held a sleeping infant in her arms.

"Is she still sleeping?" asked her husband.

"That's why she's in my arms. You know she never comes to me at all," the wife answered.

There was a look of frustration in her eyes as if she had reached the end of her patience. Both of them looked down at the beautiful baby, blissfully asleep with a serene expression on her face. The little baby had captured their hearts and become the centre of their existence. She had the face of an angel with thick, curly hair, large eyes and an ethereal quality. But her mother was at her wit's end because the baby would never come to her. As soon as she took her in her arms, the baby would start sobbing. The mother longed to play with her daughter, cradle her and cuddle her lovingly. After all she was her mother, had given birth to her and loved her more than anybody on earth. But somehow that just didn't happen.

The eyes twitched and the mouth curved upwards as if in a slight smile. Then a little hand moved up and the baby tucked it under her cheek. The expression changed and the face looked woeful as if the baby was seeing a sad dream.

"I wonder what is going on in the little mind of hers," mused the father ,"I wish she could speak and share her thoughts."

The little baby was lost in a dream world. Scenes flew in front of her eyes, scenes which made perfect sense to her, which she understood instinctively. She did not need any learning, her baby mind understood perfectly.

She saw herself as a six year old sitting in a flower bedecked hall. Her beloved father was sitting next to a lady dressed in a red and shimmering saree, laden with jewels. Her face was hidden by a veil. A priest was chanting a holy prayer and making offerings to the sacred fire.

Snatches of conversations could be heard. "So sad to lose her mother at such an early age."

"It's lucky her father found Radha. She will be a good mother to her."

"Yes, it's a second chance in life."

The scene faded away and this time the baby saw herself as a ten year old sitting next to a little boy. She saw Radha her stepmothers, giving a biscuit to the child, but none to her.

"Can I have one please?" she asked hesitatingly.

"Have you done the work I asked you to do?" Radha screamed at her with fury written on her face. Tears came into her eyes. She had never felt so alone, unloved and unwanted.

If only Papa was home, he would give her as many biscuits as she wanted.

The baby moved uncomfortably in her mother's arms. "I think she is going to wake up" murmured her father.

"Be prepared, only you can handle her," his wife whispered.

"I wonder why…"

The baby, lost in her dream world, saw her father looking extremely upset and bewildered. "I can't believe that Sumi has stolen money. Why should she? She knows she only has to ask me" he said in anguish. Radha dominated the scene, "I have told you so many times that Sumi has developed bad habits and you would never believe me. See, the hundred rupee note was in her pocket. The proof is in front of your eyes." Sumi was sobbing brokenheartedly. "I don't know how the money came in my pocket. Papa, please believe me, I haven't done anything wrong." She looked up and saw her little step brother smirking. He enjoyed seeing her in trouble. She looked pleadingly at Radha, but she could see only hatred in her eyes, eyes that looked as if they would devour her…

The bus jolted and the baby woke up with a start. In the unfocused way babies have, she looked around. As she looked upwards she saw her mother's face with the same eyes, Radha's eyes, looking down at her with hatred. She started sobbing, "Leave me alone, I haven't done anything wrong," her soul cried out in pain. Her sobs made no sense to her parents. The baby's cries increased in volume until she became almost hysterical.

"Take her!" her mother said exasperatedly. "Only then will she be quiet. God alone knows what baggage of *karma* I am carrying."

"Hush, sweetheart," her father said gently.

The baby, on hearing her father's voice, stretched out her arms towards him, arched her back and almost leapt into his arms. When she saw the eyes of her beloved father, she felt reassured and her cries became muffled. The father gave a weary sigh and lovingly cradled his daughter in his arms. He spoke in a soft soothing voice telling her how much he loved her, until she was comforted. As if the sun moved out from behind a dark cloud, her face lit up and she smiled a beautiful baby smile and cooed to her dad.

Passengers could only stare at the perfect picture they made, father and daughter in joyful, non-verbal communication with each other.

❏ ❏ ❏

16

Alone Again?

Shenaz A. Setna

It was an unusually cool Saturday morning, and the sharp breeze from the incoming high tide lent a welcoming crispness to the air. Natasha switched off the car air-conditioner and pressed the lever to lower the window as she drove down the sea-face road, to enjoy the bracing sea-breeze ruffling her hair. She expertly maneuvered her shiny new car into the limited car-parking space at her workplace, reached for her bag and briefcase and walked into her office, smiling and wishing all the staff good morning on her way.

After settling down at her desk, she switched on the computer and fished her phone out of the cavernous depths of her bag. As she checked her calls and messages, her eyebrows went up in surprise. Darius had called her twice in an hour and that too, during his working hours? He was notoriously stingy with his time, money, attention and calls. She had spent the last weekend alone, reflecting over her so-called relationship with him. "Relationship?" she wondered and smiled wryly to herself. That would be a gross over-statement, since they had been introduced a few months ago, and had been pestered, coerced and persuaded into going out with each other. She must have gone out on dates with him about half a dozen times and with his gang of friends a couple of times. Unfortunately, the time spent with each other was not very enjoyable and just a couple of shades above endurable. She felt a shudder go through her; did she want to spend any more time in her life with such a self-absorbed, self-centered person? She wanted to be loved, valued and cherished for herself, and was quite sure he would never ever do so.

She was awakened from her private reverie by the musical ring of her cell phone. Third time? Darius? She was a trifle alarmed as she picked up and answered the call.

"Natasha?" Darius's clipped cool voice came down the line. "About tonight's concert, there's a slight change!" Natasha's heart sank into her boots and her stomach felt heavy, this didn't bode well. "I've been appointed to the managing committee that's organizing today's concert. So, I will have to go in early to the venue, you will have to go there on your own. Give me a missed call when you come in, I'll give you your pass then. I'll need a lift back with you though, bye!" and the line went dead.

Natasha was furious. She had been looking forward to attending this event and was very pleased when Darius had obtained two passes from his company's sponsorship quota. She sent him a message asking him for the seat numbers and they revealed their location; a few rows from the rear and next to the wall of the auditorium. She made a note of them in her diary, and resumed her work. She was not amused.

Just after lunch, as she was rummaging around in her desk drawer, to find something important that as usual wouldn't be found easily; her eye fell upon a thick buff envelope. She pulled it out, opened the envelope and let out a gasp of surprise and a yelp of delight. Her eyes sparkled and shone with unholy glee. It was an invitation to the same concert from one of her clients, who knew that both she and her father enjoyed western classical music. She looked at it carefully and observed that it was for one person only and the seat was in a prime location. Daddy dearest was out of town visiting his precious son. How lucky was she? She waved it around with a little flourish as she carefully put it in her handbag.

The rest of the day whirred by. Natasha took a lot of care to get ready. As she slid into the driver's seat, she double-checked her purse to ensure that her precious invitation and ticket were safely tucked away.

The foyer of the Tata theatre was buzzing with people. She looked around for Darius, but there was no sign of him. She found a place to sit down and gave him a call. He told her that he was at the bar and asked her to meet him there. He was leaning on the bar, amongst a group of people, managing to look hassled and bored at the same time. She tapped him on the shoulder, and he turned around and introduced her by her name only to his colleagues. She noted that he did not mention that she was his girlfriend or even a friend. A few seconds later, he whispered into her ear, "You go ahead and sit down, here's your pass,—I'll come in later. I have to still do stuff and this is not my type of thing. Some of the guys and I are going to relax at the bar and grab a few drinks. I'll get a chance to network. I'll see you at the end!"

Natasha was aghast and growled quietly back at him. "You mean to say that I will be sitting alone, by myself for the entire concert?"

Darius just shrugged, and remarked "You'll enjoy it, maybe we can meet at the interval, but don't forget that I'll need a ride back." He grinned. "Mr. Sen, the MD brought me here in his Mercedes." He turned away and rejoined his group.

Natasha was speechless. She felt both humiliated and enraged. She turned on her heel, stumbled and was saved from falling to the floor by an arm that shot out of nowhere to grab hers. She looked up and her heart did a flip. The owner of the arm gave her a dimpled smile and then disappeared into the crush of people advancing to enter the auditorium. As she went along with the crowd, a glint of mischief entered her eyes. She shoved Darius's ticket into her bag and brought out her client's invitation and ticket. As she settled into her seat, she observed that she would be enjoying a very good view of the stage. She found a few acquaintances seated around her, and chatted with them briefly, till the bell rung.

It had been a beautiful evening, thought Natasha, as she made her way out of the theatre and down the stairs towards the car-park when Darius suddenly surfaced beside her. "I'm just chatting with my boss for a few minutes; I'll come out on the main road after you give me a buzz on the cell!" He disappeared again.

Natasha gaped in horror. The sheer effrontery of the man! As she click-clacked her way to her car, she came to a decision. She got into her car and took the exit straight onto Marine Drive and headed directly for her home.

A couple of signals ahead, her cell phone rang. She ignored it a couple of times, thinking it may be Darius, but replied when it rang the third time as she saw that it was her friend Anil and not Darius. "Where are you Nats?" he bellowed out. "We're at Sampan—the new Chinese place at Churchgate. Join us! Hurry, we're hungry!"

"Coming, on my way." The signal turned green and she hung up.

She smiled as she managed to maneuver her car and take the right turn to Churchgate. She found the restaurant easily, and oh! the privilege of valet parking! Thank God for her friends, now she wouldn't have to eat her dinner alone on a Saturday night.

"Hi Nats, how have you been? All dressed up?" cried out Ayesha, Anil's girlfriend. 'Meet Sameera, my cousin, and her boyfriend Ali. "Sameera turned around to greet her, and they both let out loud squeals of recognition and delight. "St. Xavier's? Debate and drama club?" They soon were gossiping away and catching up with each other's lives.

As they made their way through their dinner, Sameera nearly got poked in the eye by a very excited Anil, who was waving around his pair of chopsticks and yelling in his usual style, "Behram-*bawa*, where have you been?"

A shiny head turned and then a big belly followed, preceding the rest of the body, as a very plump and half-bald man waddled his way to their table. He was not so young and not so old, but his smile lit up his face and made him seem like Santa Claus. Anil gestured at him with his chopsticks again, this time narrowly missing Ali's ear. "Hey guys, this is Behram, my old school and college friend. He got up, grabbed a chair from an adjoining table and patted it. "Join us, bawa!" and pushed him down on it.

"*Arre*, my cousin is around somewhere-we went to get a drink as we had to wait for a table. Got late at the concert." Behram looked around the restaurant.

"Were you at the Tata theatre tonight?" piped in Natasha. He nodded and then smiled and waved his arm at somebody. Natasha was about to discuss the concert with him, when she looked up and nearly dropped her chopsticks. There he was! The same mop of dark brown curls atop that handsome face with that dimpled smile and twinkling grey eyes and her heart did it again. She could only stare, with her mouth slightly agape.

"This is my cousin Sam," boomed out Behram. "He's a pilot, come for a short holiday to visit his folks." Sam smiled at her, whispered to Behram, who whispered to Anil. A short game of musical chairs ensued and there he was sitting opposite her at the long table squashed between Behram and Sameera. Natasha didn't even notice Anil and Sameera smirking at her.

The night progressed and Natasha felt that she was floating on air. Sam had asked her to dance a few times on the small dance floor of the restaurant, drawing her close for the slower dances. The night drew to an end and they exchanged telephone numbers as they all settled the bill. Behram and Sam insisted on escorting her home, driving behind her in another car. Sam came right up to her front door, wished her goodnight with a light kiss on her cheek and a promise to meet the next day.

Just before she was about to retire to bed for the night, Natasha checked her phone. There were a couple of missed calls and two very angry messages from Darius. It was now past midnight. She yawned, grinned and picked up the phone and texted back. "Went alone to concert, sat alone, spent the interval alone, left theatre alone. Not alone any more. Good night and good bye, N!"

❏ ❏ ❏

17

Chrysalis

Rita Chhablani

New Delhi

Seema stretched her arms and looked around her at her gilded cage. Slowly, she got out of bed. It was late, for as soon as she opened the curtains, the sun, hot and angry came streaming into the room. Startled, she looked at the time. It was nearly 10 am. Usually she was an early riser, but with nothing to do, why wake up early?

Akash, her dear husband had literally deposited her in the fancy company guest house in Maharani Bagh, a posh suburb of Delhi and had pushed off the very next morning on one of his exhaustive fortnight-long tours. She was left twiddling her thumbs with only the portrait-lined walls for company and an extremely talented but arrogant boor of a *khansama* who, she had to confess, turned out the most delectable food.

At first, she had enjoyed this lotus eater kind of life style, loved exploring the fancy mansion, gingerly touching its unique artifacts and antiques. It was such luxury after the tough grind her life had been in Mumbai, juggling both career and home. Akash had been offered this plum assignment as Vice President of a start-up IT company.

"Soon, we will be rich beyond compare!" He had burst into the house, brimming with excitement, after the interview with the top management based in Palo Alto, in the US. "One day Google or Microsoft will buy us out! You understand what that means? For me, for us?" He had all but begged, cupping her face, looking into her eyes, willing her into agreeing.

Against her will, she had given in, sacrificing her career in favour of his. This was the story of her life. Her name meant *'limit'* and so it had been, starting with her childhood, she had unquestioningly walked the path laid down by her parents. A barrier had been built around her, one she dare not cross, even in her dreams. All the time it had been, "Do this," and "Don't do that." This from her caring and so–called emancipated father. Or, at least, so she had thought he was.

And from her mother, the epitome of an obedient wife, it was always about, "Good girls do not speak loudly," "Good girls must do this or do that." As she grew into adolescence, the boundaries had only become tighter. And stifling!

And then she, had married Akash. Did his name not mean the skies; unhindered, limitless? Boundary married to the boundless! She had been excited. For the first time, she had felt she had a chance to get away from her cage and take flight.

But she had realized, soon after, that he had continued to encage her. "I do not want my wife to while away her time with empty gossip and become a housewife," he had said firmly to her, when all she had looked forward to was being his wife. But no, he wanted a career for her, and so it had to be.

No questions asked, she had set out to find a job, and to her happy surprise, she had found one soon enough in the HR department of a reputed advertising company. She had worked hard and her sincere attitude and merit had caught the attention of the big bosses. They had wanted to promote her to a position where she would have to travel.

Once again, there had appeared that wall, she had so dreaded. "This far and no further," said Akash. "I do not want our home to suffer." So, she had tried to be happy in her humble position.

After a few years of marriage, she had wanted children. Her dear husband, however, had not wanted to be encumbered by any such obstacles. "It will distract you from your job," he said.

Such had been her life so far! She sighed, as she entered the guest house library one day during her voyage of discovery. From the rows of books lining the well polished oak wood cabinets, she scanned and picked up one of the classics, and settled down on a cane chair placed on the well manicured lawns. It was such a luxury to be able to read a book. Soon, she was lost in time and place, until an irritating intrusion marred her attention. It was the bearer who appeared to place wafer-thin cucumber sandwiches and hot coffee on the table beside her.

She continued to be lost in the world of Jane Austen, until her hand of its own accord, reached out and she took a bite of the delectable melt-in-the mouth sandwich. Now, she needed a sip of the coffee, the aroma of which was fast becoming irresistible. She lay down her book for a while. No point trying so hard to juggle between two such tempting activities. Life had been a tough grind back in Mumbai. This was heaven.

The only problem here was, there was no one for company. Not a soul around. Here, she was the queen of the lonely castle. It was boring, this lotus-eater's existence.

She decided this was an opportunity to sharpen her next to zero culinary skills. A few days later, she followed the direction from where a delicious aroma was wafting to her nostrils and she reached the kitchen. Standing at the threshold, she could see a white-haired man, stirring something so intently in a pot on the cooking range, as though he was doing his thesis.

Finding courage, she cleared her throat and asked a trifle hesitantly, trying hard to inject some friendliness in her voice, "What are you making, *khansamaji?* I love the food you cook. Can you... uhh... teach me? I am alone."

The dour-faced, aproned cook looked up condescendingly from his task and cast such a scornful look at her that she shrank back, horrified to see the fire emanating from his eyes. She at once realized she had made a dreadful mistake. She had stepped into forbidden territory, right into the dragon's lair and she made a quick getaway.

Same story with the washerwoman, with whom she tried to pick up some conversation. She was the cook's wife and equally foul-tempered. The gardener who kept such an excellent garden... same story. What was it about this guest house? What was wrong with people here?

'Thank God,' she sighed, 'this was a temporary accommodation, till they found a rental place of their own.' She prayed it would be soon after Akash's return. Then, she would try to find a job.

'Till then, maybe the world of books would have to suffice,' she thought, flipping the pages of Gulliver's Travels, which she had picked up this time, one of her favourite books in school. She sat lost in the world of fantasy.

Suddenly, the sound of laughter broke into her thoughts. Confused, she looked around. It seemed as though a child's innocent squeals were coming from a distance. She got up and decided to sleuth around. For the first time since she had come to this place, she went to the gate and fumbled with the latch.

A small click and it opened wide and she stepped out into the street. To her surprise, she saw a park located right outside the guest house. Hesitantly, she entered through a small gate and lo and behold, an entirely new world opened before her. It had been right here, waiting for her all these days, when she had been getting bored and wallowing in self pity, beating her head against those arrogant boors, the cook and the gardener, so insecure in their positions.

She took a deep breath. It was like she had walked into Aladdin's cave...the blue open skies, the chirping of a variety of birds fluttering around, flowers of all hues blooming profusely and old people sitting on benches chatting away, without a care in the world. "Open *Sim-sim*," is all that it had needed.

But where was that laughter that had attracted her here, in the first place ?

And then she saw *him*! It was a little boy, with a dirt streaked face, wearing torn but clean clothes, standing near a tree. Not wanting to scare him, she tiptoed and stood behind him, trying to see what he was watching with such concentration that was amusing him so. And, then, her eyes descended on a chrysalis and there was something emerging from within... the caterpillar was trying to break it open. She too, like the boy, stood with bated breath, waiting and watching for the miracle to happen.

Within seconds, there emerged from the dark confinement the most brilliant butterfly. It fluttered its wings for a moment.

This sudden action startled the boy. He stepped back and fell right on Seema, who was standing behind him, watching wonder-struck.

Seema lost her balance and fell back on the softness of the green grass, the little boy on top of her, both awe-struck watching the butterfly flitting away towards its freedom. It was gone, and now the boy turned back and looked with surprise at Seema.

Seeing her expression, he burst once again into those delightful peals of laughter that had led Seema here in the first place. She, to her surprise, began giggling like a little child too.

She held the boy tight, thankful for this precious moment he had given her. A minute later, he rolled away in happy abandon and she couldn't help but follow.

A short while later, they lay quiet and exhausted and silent as Seema looked up at the vastness of the blue skies, at the innumerable small white clouds passing by, like delicate will o'wisps.

The boy stood up and said to her, "Come, I want you to meet somebody." He extended a hand and she, usually rational and careful by nature, spontaneously jumped up. There had been something in the boy's eyes.

He led her to the farthest corner of the garden where there was a yoga session in progress.

"Madam," he called out to the smart attractive woman who was the leader. Seema tried to stop the boy from disturbing the class and pulled him away. To her surprise the woman, said, "Excuse me," got up at once, came towards them and enveloped the boy in a hug.

"Yes, Siddharth, what is it?" she asked most lovingly.

That was the name of Buddha! It did not surprise Seema, for hadn't the boy brought such joy in her life. She was surprised, however, to see the love and the glow on this woman's face, The energy radiating from her, It simply stunned her.

"Madam, I want you to meet my new friend," said the boy simply.

"If my little friend wants me to meet you, I must," the woman said, extending her hand towards Seema. "I am Sulbha," she said simply.

"I am Seema," said Seema shyly, a little hesitantly, afraid to step over the *limit* she was conditioned to. But there was something about the other woman's warmth and candour that probably disarmed her.

Over the next few days, Sulbha took her under her wing and exposed her to the joys of yoga and meditation and introduced her to the world of street children, of which Siddharth was one.

A week later, on her way back to the guest house after a long, tiring but satisfying day of teaching in one of the thatched huts of a slum close by, Seema thought, Siddhartha had truly proved to be the little Buddha for her. It was he, who had given her the magic words, "*Khul ja Sim-sim... Open Sesame...*" and opened this magical world for her.

She felt like that butterfly that had emerged from its cocoon. Suddenly, the words flashed through her mind… "Just when the caterpillar thought it's life was over, it began to fly." She had been born again... thanks to Siddarth who had been her catalyst and led her to Sulbha. For the first time, Seema felt she had found her purpose in life.

It was her secret, one her husband must not know, for he would never understand. In easy languor, she sat devouring the soft yummy lightly spiced cauliflower *paranthas* with a delectable North Indian style mango pickle and creamy cucumber *raita*. She was hungry. Now she no longer held a grudge against the cook or the gardener. Her rancour, her bitterness had long since vanished. She reclined back in the cane chair, and looked at the unhindered boundless skies. When would her husband, Akash become true to his name? Why was he always so *limiting*?

A fortnight later, all hell broke loose, when she returned to the guest house, after a lovely afternoon. Sulbha had invited her to her exquisite home for lunch and she had met her distinguished husband, a well-known psychiatrist. She admired him for letting his wife be who she was, instead of confining her, in his own insecurity. They were made-for-each-other, both reveling in each other's freedom. For the first time, she understood what a true marriage was, a union of minds and hearts and bodies. With a glass of wine, they had celebrated the success of one of their protégés. The student had topped the board exams and all the others had cleared the same, as well.

"*Sahib* is back," the cook said, as soon as he saw her. "He is upstairs and asked where you were."

That was enough to send her scampering to their bedroom, where Akash was waiting, his face red with anger. "Where have you been gallivanting while I work my butt off?" he thundered.

"Only when you calm down, will I tell you," she stated matter of factly, without any fear, surprisingly

She could see Akash stare at her with amazement, wondering, confused at this change in her. He was about to repeat his question, when he saw the look in her eyes and he changed tactics, She knew him too well. He was a man who had been spoilt,used to getting his own way, by any means.

Sure enough, he fell on the bed, clutching the region of his heart, moaning with pain.

Seema rolled her eyes and instead of rushing to him, as she always did, she dialed Sulbha's number quickly. The two friends had discussed the plan, in case such an exigency developed.

"Whom are you calling?" asked her husband from the bed, groaning, rubbing his chest.

"The doctor," she stated simply.

He barked, "Why? I do not need one."

"No, you need one, you could be having an attack," she remarked, wanting to catch him on his bluff.

Few minutes later, Sulbha and her husband, Mahesh, walked into the room.

One look at the man lying on the bed and Sulbha burst out, "You Akash! Here after all these years!"

Akash gaped at the attractive woman and then exclaimed,

"Sulbha! Right? Am I hallucinating? After all these years? Where did you vanish? I missed you. You! A doctor? How does Seema know you?"

"*Dramebaaz* as always, not changed one bit, you naughty boy," Sulbha scolded him, boxing him on his chest. "Now sit up and stop troubling this poor girl, my dear friend, or else I will tell my doctor husband to give you an injection."

A few minutes later, over a steaming cup of tea and some fresh oven-baked biscuits, came out a tender childhood tale.

"Sulbha was my best friend's older sister. Our parents owned the adjacent coffee estates in Coonoor," Akash told his audience.

"And this naughty boy in his leather jacket was forever zooming by on his powerful motor bike on those narrow roads. Scaring the chickens and later the pretty chicks, literally! Quite a charmer he was, and a heart breaker," teased Sulbha.

"You were my ideal," said Akash, looking adoringly like a little boy at the older, elegant woman. "After you married, you just vanished out of my life. I missed you."

"Your wife is a very dear friend and she is doing such noble work, you should be proud of her," Sulbha said to him. "And young man, you need to pitch in too."

At that moment, Seema felt a change. Some of her limits had lifted further.

***

A few months later Seema and Akash moved into a lovely flat in Gurgaon. They threw a housewarming party where they also invited their dear friends Sulbha and Mahesh, some special street children, the volunteers involved in the project and some of Akash's office colleagues.

"Surprise," announced Akash, welcoming a young man

who had walked in. "Seema, meet my boss, Atul. He wants to talk to Sulbha and you about a proposal he has for your street children project."

Sulbha and Seema stared at each other across the room with joy-filled eyes. They were ready.

Soon, laughter and joy filled the room The children left soon after bursting balloons. Delectable appetizers and drinks did the rounds. The adults sat, nursing their glasses and watching the evening lights dotting the horizon.

Akash's fingers found Seema's and held them tight. She looked at him and smiled and naughtily blew a kiss at him. She had come a long way. From its claustrophobic, cocooned life, the caterpillar within her had burst out as a butterfly. She was ready to fly into the freedom of the boundless skies.

The *"limited"* Seema and Akash, the *'limitless'* skies had finally merged.

❏ ❏ ❏

18

Give Love a Second Chance

Jayashree Dhillon

He saw her swimming in the pool in neat, effortless strokes. She waited at the shallow end for a few moments, smiled at the kids splashing about and then with one graceful movement pulled herself out of the water. 'Hmm, good figure… and great legs,' he thought to himself.

She sauntered across to the vacant chair next to him, picked up her towel and lowered herself into the chair. He thought he should introduce himself. "Hi, I am Major Ajay Rathore. Recently posted here in Pune."

"Hello, I am Aditi," she smiled in return and looked at the person sitting next to her. She saw a friendly smile, deep dimples and a strong jaw.

"Do you come here often?" he asked. "I am new to Pune and would love to make some friends."

"I am visiting my parents. They live here," replied Aditi, taking a sip from her glass of *nimbu-pani*.

Minutes flew by as Ajay threw a barrage of questions at her. "What do you do? Are you working? Where do you live? Will you show me around the city?"

Acutely conscious of the handsome stranger's gaze on her exposed honey coloured skin, Aditi got up suddenly and said, "I better go. I have to pick up a few things from the coffee shop. Do excuse me. Nice meeting you."

"Hey, wait a minute! Maybe you can introduce me to the goodies in the coffee shop," said Ajay.

'What a persistent fellow,' thought Aditi as she walked to the changing room. She changed into a hip-hugging pair of Levis and a crisp, white cotton T-shirt, collected her bag and walked out. Sure enough, Ajay was waiting by the poolside.

They walked to the coffee shop. Aditi placed her order and helped Ajay choose a few delicious looking pastries.

"Sweets for the sweet," said Ajay, as he dropped a small packet of chocolates into Aditi's hands.

"Oh no! I couldn't take these," exclaimed Aditi.

"Of course, you could! You seem to have tried everything in this place. Don't tell me you don't like chocolates? And now for being such a help, allow me to buy you a coffee," said Ajay, ignoring Aditi's protests and leading her to an empty table, while balancing a cup of coffee in each hand. Aditi sat down resignedly. She had to admit to herself that Ajay was quite a flirt, but she was enjoying the attention.

Half an hour later Aditi glanced at her watch. "Oh my gosh, just look at the time! I am horribly late. I better run. Thanks for the coffee." Aditi hurried to the door.

Ajay called after her, "See you at the pool tomorrow."

Aditi said over her shoulder, "I don't swim every day," and with a wave of her hand she was gone.

Driving back, Aditi thought to herself. 'Ajay had been very charming but how could she have allowed herself to have a coffee and spend so much time with him? God knows she enjoyed his company, his banter, even his flirting.'

Maybe, after months of a hectic work schedule in an ad agency in Mumbai, she needed that break. Her thoughts came back to the present as she reached her house.

Rahul would be waiting for her after his game of cricket. Suddenly, she felt very guilty.

***

A couple of weeks later...

It was the May Queen Ball at the club. Crowds of well-dressed men and women were milling around. The band belted out popular numbers. The club building, trees and shrubs were decorated with tiny, twinkling lights. It was a glittering evening. Aditi was looking absolutely stunning in a black clingy dress. Sequins sparkled on her dress and on her sleeves. A double strand of glistening pearls adorned her neck. Small solitaires flashed in her ears. Her thick wavy hair fell about her shoulders in abundance. She was watching the fashion show, when a deep male voice said to her, "Well, well, well. Look who's here? Where have you been hiding Aditi? I was disappointed at not seeing you at the pool. But let's make up for lost time." It was Ajay. The fashion show ended and the compere announced the next dance. "Come on, let's dance," said Ajay, expertly leading Aditi to the floor. Aditi felt herself relax and surrender to the beat of the music. After a couple of dances, they were thirsty and went to get a drink.

The music changed to slow numbers. Back on the floor, Aditi was extremely conscious of Ajay's closeness. He held her hand and encircled her small waist with his other arm. A shiver ran down her back at his touch. 'Behave yourself, girl!' Aditi admonished herself mentally. But she would be a liar, if she said she wasn't getting attracted to Ajay Rathore. "I am tired," announced Aditi, a few dances later.

"Let's pick up a drink and go to the terrace. It will be cooler there after the crowds on the dance floor," said Ajay.

They stood near the parapet wall on the terrace, in companionable silence. It was a warm night but a soft breeze was blowing. The heady fragrance of jasmine and *raat-ki-rani*, was wafting up from the club garden. The sky was a velvety black, with a bright full moon drenching everything in a silvery light. It was a magical night.

Ajay was standing so close to Aditi that he could smell her perfume. He was feeling intoxicated. He didn't know if it was the whiskey or her perfume but he had this uncontrollable urge to hold her and kiss her. 'Dear God! Don't let me spoil this,' he thought to himself. He tossed down the whiskey in one big gulp.

"You drink too fast," scolded Aditi.

"I know," Ajay replied. "But it helps to pass long evenings and longer nights when you are alone, somewhere at a border post. It also helps to dull the pain of a broken heart."

Aditi looked at him sharply. 'Was this, was all this 'chasing her' on the rebound then?' she thought but she heard herself saying, "Would you like to talk about it?"

"Some other time," Ajay whispered, "let us just enjoy the moment."

The spell was broken and Aditi said, "It's getting late. I must get back." Again, Aditi felt guilty about Rahul. She had to tell Ajay about Rahul but felt that it was not the right time.

"Come, I'll walk you to your table," Ajay offered.

Aditi introduced Ajay to her parents and their friends who were sitting around at their table. Aditi's father, an affable person, had retired from the Army as a Colonel and now worked for an IT company. Her mother, an elegant lady, was a freelance writer for several women's magazines. Colonel Malhotra took to Ajay right away. He pumped Ajay's hand vigorously, patted him on the back and said, "Here is my card young man. Give me a call if you want to play a game of tennis or a round of golf. I may have retired but I am certainly not down and out."

"Thank you, Sir. I will take you up on that. Breakfast and beer will be on me after the game," answered Ajay, delighted with the invitation.

The next morning, the shrill ring of the phone disturbed the peace and quiet of the Malhotra household. The Colonel answered the phone, spoke for a few minutes and came grinning into Aditi's room. "Your young man obviously prefers you over me. Major Ajay Rathore wants to talk to you!"

Aditi's heart gave a little flutter and quite unable to conceal her happiness, she hurried to take Ajay's call. She picked up the receiver and with her other hand, gently pushed the door of the room shut, to ensure herself some privacy. "Hello, good morning," she whispered into the phone. She hoped Ajay wouldn't hear the thudding of her heart. What was the matter with her? This was totally out of character.

"Hi!" Ajay's rich voice came across to her. "I hope you have surfaced after the late night. I couldn't sleep a wink."

"Why?" asked Aditi, with a tremble in her voice. She had been tossing and turning in her bed all night herself!

Ajay replied in a soft even voice, "I have been thinking about you. About us. I don't want to lose you Aditi. Let's get married."

Completely thrown off guard, Aditi was at a loss for words. Why couldn't she find something smart to say? "Married! But we have just met a couple of times... you hardly know me," whispered Aditi into the phone.

"Then give me a chance to find out," Ajay replied. "Let's meet for dinner. I will pick..." Aditi cut him short.

"I can't, I am sorry. I am catching the early morning train to Mumbai tomorrow. I have a presentation at 11:30... an important client. I have to be there."

"I don't care. Cancel the meeting. Report sick...," said Ajay recklessly. "This is about us together Aditi."

"I really can't Ajay. I am sorry," insisted Aditi.

"All right then Aditi, I am picking you up today around noon. We will have lunch together. See you." Ajay sounded like a sullen child.

From then on, Aditi was as if in a trance. A million thoughts flashed through her mind. 'He is talking marriage. What do I know about him? What does he know about me? I haven't told him about Rahul.' For the umpteenth time she felt guilty.

Aditi was barely ready, when Ajay's car swerved into the porch. She was dressed casually in a pretty, pink floral shirt, teamed with off-white pants. A single pearl adorned each of her ear lobes. Strappy white sandals, matching a large, white hand bag, completed her outfit.

Aditi slid into the car. The two of them exchanged 'hellos'. Ajay looked distraught, his face almost ashen. They drove in silence. Just to break the ice, Aditi said, "Where are we going?"

Ajay replied, "You decide, I am new around here."

Aditi said, "Not to a fancy place I hope, I am dressed too casually."

"You are looking good enough to eat," smiled Ajay at last. "Any place is good enough, as long as we can sit down and talk undisturbed."

All the way to the restaurant, Aditi wondered, 'How will he react when I tell him about Rahul? What will he think of me?'

Lunch was a quiet affair with both of them picking at their food. Mid-way through their meal, Ajay covered Aditi's hand with his and said, "Let's get married Aditi. Like I said earlier, I don't want to lose you."

Aditi tried to pull her hand away, though she knew she didn't want to. "All this is so sudden Ajay. I haven't really thought of marriage. We have hardly met a couple of times. You are a warm, wonderful person, great company and I really like you. But marriage? I don't know much about you," Aditi managed to say.

"So, what do you want to know?" asked Ajay. "Okay. I will tell you about myself. My family is from Rajasthan. My father is a retired Brigadier settled in Jaipur. At a very young age I was sent off to boarding school. Next, came the National Defence Academy, then the Indian Military Academy. After that I joined the infantry – same regiment as my father's. Holidays back home were spent in the company of cousins and friends. One of them was Vasundhara. I always had a crush on her. She was a childhood friend. We grew up together. She was from a royal family. Everyone expected us to marry. Yes, we were good friends but as we grew up, Vasu realised she preferred the high society life to being an army officer's wife. At least she was honest about it. We were both very young. Anyway, all this was many years ago. Nothing serious after that. Any other questions?" Ajay ended his monologue.

"Ajay… " Aditi hesitated. "You don't know anything about me… "

"I know enough," Ajay cut into her sentence. "You are a smart, good looking woman. Well- educated, who works and lives alone in Mumbai. An independent woman. I admire that. You swim, play tennis and go trekking. I like a sporty, outdoorsy woman. We have similar interests. I have met your parents. They are warm and cultured people. Most importantly, we get along famously and enjoy each other's company."

"But Ajay…" Aditi still hesitated.

"What is it Aditi? Is there someone else?" Ajay asked, his voice barely audible.

Aditi had to summon all her courage to tell Ajay the truth. "Ajay, I have to tell you about Rahul…"

Ajay looked at her sharply but keeping his voice steady said "So tell me. Who is Rahul?"

Aditi replied in an equally steady voice, "My son."

Ajay was stunned. He wasn't sure that he had heard right. He felt a sudden wrench in his heart. "Your son?"

"Yes, my son," Aditi replied. She felt as if a burden had lifted from her shoulders. "I have been married before… Rahul is my eight-year-old son. He lives here with my parents. They have virtually brought him up."

Ajay took a few deep breaths to calm himself and said gently, "Would you like to talk about it?"

Before she knew it, Aditi heard herself telling Ajay all about Ronnie and herself.

Aditi and Ronnie's parents were friends and neighbours in the army accommodation in Delhi. So naturally, the children also became friends. Ronnie, the eldest son, was studying in a well-known public school in Mussourie and would come down to Delhi for his holidays. Aditi and Ronnie were the same age. They got along well and became good friends. They would write to each other when they were apart. Soon, Ronnie finished school and joined St. Stephens College in Delhi. Aditi joined Miranda House. They had a lot more time to spend with each other. Movies, picnics, parties and dances–Ronnie and Aditi were always together. They became inseparable. Their friendship blossomed into love and they announced to their parents that they wanted to marry. The parents were aghast as their children were barely nineteen years old! Never mind a job, neither of them even had a college degree.

The parents tried to reason with them but it was no use. The kids threatened to run away and get married. So Aditi and Ronnie were married in a simple ceremony and they moved in with Ronnie's parents. Their fights started soon after the wedding. Both of them were very young and immature, not ready to shoulder the responsibility of a marriage. A son was born to them after a year. Aditi just could not manage the baby. Both Ronnie and Aditi were fed up and decided to separate. The parents too, agreed to this. The divorce, by mutual consent came through pretty quickly. Aditi got the custody of her son Rahul, as he was still a small child.

Aditi was crying uncontrollably by now. Ajay offered her his hanky. She took it, dabbed her eyes, had a sip of water and continued, "I went back to my parents and started life from scratch. I completed my degree, then my post-graduation. I had to settle myself and stand on my own feet. I did a course in advertising and public relations and after a string of poorly paid jobs, eventually got a good break in Mumbai."

In between sobs, Aditi continued, "My parents have been my only support. They have brought up Rahul since the time he was a year old. He is all I have. I feel so guilty living away from him but… but it is impossible for me to look after him… alone in a city like Mumbai. I have a demanding job and work long hours most days." Aditi burst into tears again. A few minutes later, she struggled to regain her composure and said in an exhausted voice, "Forgive me Ajay, if you can. I should have told you everything last night at the dance. But I was having such a wonderful time after ages, I didn't want to spoil it. I am sorry, so sorry."

Aditi picked up her bag and stood up to leave.

"Where do you think you are going?" asked Ajay.

"I need to get home," replied Aditi, "If you don't want to see me after this… I'll understand."

"Dear girl!" exclaimed Ajay. "I can't let you walk out of my life just like that. Calm down, freshen up and I will take you home." He smiled and added, "I have to make friends with Rahul!"

❏ ❏ ❏

19

The Matchmaker

Manjula Shukla

"Sharad is late again," I thought with a sigh. The clock had struck nine o'clock. "Drat his boss, how he drives my boy. He's so overworked and exhausted." I looked hopefully towards the front door as I thought I heard a step on the landing. I waited to hear the sound of his latch key in the lock but there was no sound. Too bad, the wait was not over. The television on a timer came to life and I settled down on my comfortable but worn out rug with my eyes glued to my favourite cartoon Tom and Jerry.

It was past midnight, when the door opened and Sharad came in. He looked really tired, poor dear. His eyes were sunken and had dark shadows. The shirt which had looked smart and fresh in the morning was limp and stained with a small patch of coffee on the sleeve. Had he even had lunch, I wondered. He gave me an affectionate glance and a sincere smile of apology. I jumped up with exuberance, but seeing his fatigue, calmed down. He warmed his dinner in the microwave oven, gave me mine on my special plate and we both hit the sack.

This routine continued for quite a few days. Even weekends were not spared. There were no walks or recreation or socialization. It was either office or working from home. To top it off, were a number of conference calls where I could hear every team member complaining and the project leaders screaming. I cursed his boss innumerable times but was helpless. It was time, I decided, to take matters in my own hands.

Sharad and I had a special kind of understanding. We could tune into each other's thoughts. He knew exactly when I felt like having a snack or wanted an outing. He also knew of my unrequited love for Lily, who lived in the next block. She was of impeccable lineage, blue blood at its bluest. She was a beauty, always well turned out. There was a pink bow on the side of her head, calculated to make her admirers' hearts beat faster. When she went on her daily walk outside and paraded with mincing steps down the road, all of us were prepared to tear our hearts out for her. She, however, would trample on our feelings, ignore us with her nose up in the air and carry on without a second thought.

However, regarding my boy, I knew what was going on in his heart and mind. It was the nesting instinct created by Nature, just to complicate life. He yearned for a soul mate. His heart was heavy with longing but so far he hadn't found anyone. My heart swelled with pride. It would have to be a girl in a million to match up to him. I felt like screaming to all and sundry "Don't go by his appearance and shy manner. See his pure soul and heart of gold." But no girl would listen to me.

Seeing his pensive expression, tired eyes and killing routine, I decided enough was enough. I would search for a mate for him. But who would it be and where would I find her? No one in the vicinity was good enough for him. I had very high standards in my choice for his better half.

From that day onwards, I kept a keen lookout whenever I ventured outdoors. The fairer sex got more than one glance from me but nobody measured up. A chance meeting with my old chum Tommy gave me an opening. "The doctor's new assistant is a real dish," he chuckled. I chided him for his disrespectful manner, but it gave me a brainwave.

From the next day, I started a subterfuge. I acted lethargic, pecked at my food with loud sighs and affected a manner of extreme weariness. Sharad, at once, noted it and took me to the doctor the very next day.

The wait in the outer chamber seemed to last forever. I was feverish in my impatience and my boy thought it was because I was not feeling well. The minute I saw her, I knew she was the one. She was tall and fair with a pleasant expression. The light blue salwar suit that she was wearing suited her admirably. Her name tag read "Dr. Purnima Seth." a union made in heaven, 'Sharad' and 'Purnima', even the names matched.

She put me on the examining table, checked my temperature, pressed my abdomen, peered into my mouth and eyes and used her stethoscope to rule out congestion. Then she gave her verdict, "Doesn't seem to be serious, I'll prescribe some vitamins." I agreed with her completely. Not only was she beautiful, she was also good at her job, an ideal partner for my boy. In my excitement, I jumped off the table and almost started to dance a small jig of joy.

Sharad was transfixed at the change in me. His lines of worry eased and a wide endearing grin appeared on his face. Turning towards Dr. Purnima he smiled and said in his most charming manner, "I'm very relieved. If you are free some day, I would like to take you out for a cup of coffee to express my gratitude." She, too, smiled back and nodded. Deep dimples appeared in her cheeks and my boy was mesmerised at the sight. That was the exact moment he lost his heart. My life was made, my goal achieved. I swear I could hear the tinkle of wedding bells in the distance. I gave a heartfelt sigh and a deep "Woof, woof" as a seal of my approval.

❏ ❏ ❏

20

Cat vs. Crow!

Mala Rihan

Caw! Caw!.... Miaow…..Caw! Caw!....

At first I thought all the noise was a part of my dream and images of crows attacking a kitten had begun floating before my sleepy eyes.

The cacophony was becoming worse, rendering sleep impossible. There was a cat whose loud mewing and wailing was matched by equally loud cawing by the crows. The noise seemed to be coming from just outside my window.

"Looks like the crows are attacking a kitten," I murmured to my husband as I reluctantly pulled aside the covers and got out of the mosquito net. Sleepy eyed, I lurched to the window, and looked out at something black and shapeless like a piece of plastic fluttering near a parked car. Reaching for my glasses, I put them on to see that the fluttering object was the focus of attention of a white cat half hidden under a car and two black crows flying around, all screeching away.

"Crows and cats are having a fight," I mumbled to my husband as I slipped on a pair of shoes. I went down hurriedly and reached the scene of the big fight. It then became clear that what I had taken to be a bag of goodies was actually a baby crow.

Well it was a pretty large baby, with a very sharp pointy beak. With a wing at half mast, it was unable to fly. 'It must have fallen out of the nest and hurt itself,' I thought to myself. 'Or perhaps it had been trying out its maiden flight and had been unsuccessful. No time to worry about all that now.' It was hopping around crazily with one wing half spread out and the cat was making determined efforts to attack and drag it under the Fiat car parked there.

The parent crows were going at the cat hammer and tongs, cawing away and pecking any part that they could get at. "Touch my baby and die!" was no doubt the meaning of all that cawing. The squealing cat, however, was obviously planning a baby crow feast, so was not willing to give up.

Twin sharp beaks, and flapping wings, a white malevolent hunter with sharp teeth, paws and bad intentions, the situation called for quick and decisive action. When I came into the picture, the crows flew up to the bar of the netting surrounding a nearby play area, watching from there.

Banging hard on the Fiat door resulted in the cat scampering out towards the wall where Papa crow was all set to swoop on her. Mewing loudly, she slithered away. Further banging and out came another black and white cat, her partner in crime. Protesting loudly, this one slinked away too, realizing that the prize was no longer as attractive as it had seemed. But for how long would they be gone? They would be back the minute I left.

The crows, having achieved a minor victory, flew from their positions on the ground and netting to a higher perch on the tree. I grabbed a neighbor's newspaper and tried to get the baby to hop on to it. But it kept moving away. I spotted the *chowkidar* a short distance away and gave him a shout. "*Bhaiya*, please come here."

He strolled up at his usual pace.

"*Yeh kauve ko uthana hai,*" (we need to pick up this crow) I said, trying to recruit him to the baby's cause.

Ah, but the *chowkidar*, obviously one of a higher rank, could not be roped in to do this menial job. He called out to the gardener or *maali* who had been watering the lawn meditatively, oblivious to the noise and action.

When the *maali* came up, he was reluctant to touch the crow because he was afraid that the parents would attack him if he lifted their baby. Hop-along Cassidy was also not being very cooperative. With his long beak and claws, he looked quite menacing, while the swooping parents made it clear that they were guarding their baby with all their might.

"Here take this paper and catch him with it, I'll make sure the crows don't touch you," I said with a confidence that was convincing. The *maali* was a man of action. On my reassurance, he managed to pick up the crow in the folds of the newspaper.

Now came the question of what to do with it. Putting it back in the nest was out of the question. I doubted that the crows would allow us to do that. Leaving it on the wall or car would not keep it safe from the cats. My glance fell on the basket ball court. There was a wall separating it from the swimming pool, with a decorative part that had some plants on it, about 6 feet from the ground. Just right, I thought to myself. I indicated the space to the *maali*, who quickly deposited the bird, handed me the newspaper and left.

This proceeding was watched carefully by the parent crows, but there was no more cawing and swooping while we carried their baby to safety. With the help of my neighbor, we gave it a bowl of water and bits of bread.

Morning rescue mission over, I returned home to enjoy a hot cup of tea in my balcony, peacefully, with the remnants of the neighbors' newspaper!

The next morning I saw the adventurous baby in the swimming pool area, hopping along the sides, no doubt finding the expanse of water more soothing than the small space we had left it in. When I went for my swim, it stayed quietly on the side. The Papa and Mama crow were not to be seen. But luckily, neither were the cats. Since there were walls and greenery all along the sides of the pool, possibly the cats had not found it.

Feeding it and ensuring that it did not have to drink the chlorinated pool water, was my task for the next few days. Armed with a small packet containing some leftover goodies, and a small bottle of water to refill his bowl, I would make a daily pilgrimage to the poolside.

A few days later, the baby crow was gone. I do hope that it had become strong and the wing had mended enough for it to fly off. No one had seen it go.

21

What's His..Uh..Her Name?

Shenaz A. Setna

"Adi and Ayesha. Adi and Ayesha." If I say it aloud to myself often enough, I'll be bound to remember it.

"It's not so difficult to remember it, Sara!" says my husband Soli, peering over his glasses at me, legs up on the coffee table, head buried deep into his newspaper. "They both begin with A and it is shorter than the last one- Scherezade!"

"Yes I know!" I sigh. He puts out a hand and strokes my arm in a show of encouragement and support, but in a flash his hand and arm disappear again into the folds of his newspaper.

Blast my middle-aged memory! I can remember my own son's name-Adi- thank God, but not the name of his procession of girlfriends! His elder brother Farhad, married his college girlfriend as soon as he was settled in his job and his sister, Sanaya, married one of her work colleagues within a year of meeting him. Adi, our youngest son, recently turned thirty, but shows no sign of entering into a long term stable relationship, let alone marriage.

I don't have trouble with either my daughter-in-law's, or son-in-law's names. My son and his family are happily settled in Australia, whilst my daughter and her family relocated to

Dubai a couple of years ago. We chat regularly via Skype with them, with big white name cards next to me, thoughtfully provided by my husband, with the grandchildren's names written in bold capital letters – not so easy to remember them!

"Adi and Ayesha," I mutter to myself repeatedly as I go through my morning household chores. By lunchtime, my husband is apparently fed up and snaps at me- "Enough! It sounds like a mantra or your prayers! How come you never forget the names of the maids, the watchmen or the delivery boys, but forget my colleagues' and their spouses' names? Selective amnesia! " He ends with a growl and chomps his way through his Sunday afternoon *dhansakh*.

I sigh, he is absolutely right and I have no intention of spoiling my Sunday afternoon feast and nap with trivial bickering.

I take a deep breath and smile at him. "I've got to get it right this time Soli! I called his last girlfriend by the wrong name, and Adi was fuming. Apparently, Miss curly-hair thought he was involved with another girl. They had a huge fight and eventually broke up." I shake my head in regret.

"Do you remember Charlie?" asks my husband with a chuckle. "We both thought she was a boy and were wondering if Adi had suddenly become gay!" We both burst out laughing. "How can I forget?" I exclaim.

"Don't worry *jaanu*, he'll settle down when he finds the right girl," my husband consoles me. According to me, he already had. The only girl whose face and name I never did and never will forget – Perveen, pretty, sweet-natured and smart, with a smiling face and a saucy sense of humour that had us giggling or in splits of laughter very often. Adi was relaxed around her, and seemed very happy, until the one year deadline loomed, then he made his customary "I am not ready to commit" speech and drama and she left him for hopefully greener pastures.

We both wake up refreshed after our afternoon siesta and are sitting on the balcony, sipping our tea, when the phone rings.

"Hi Ma," come the chirpy voice of my youngest son. "There's a slight change of plans. Can we come by around six for a drink and chat, instead of the dinner at Mainland China?"

"Oh dear, Adi, the maid doesn't come in on Sunday evenings and I have nothing in the house!"

"Don't worry Ma, just order the samosas and sandwiches from Lucky and get a couple of pastries or cake from the bakery. Don't get beer, she doesn't like it. Bye!" The line went dead.

"They are coming at six instead! Typical of him, I've only got an hour to get things ready!" My voice became a bit shrill with irritation and panic.

Soli raises his left eyebrow, just like Adi. Like father, like son, or was it the other way around? He never did it until Adi started it. "Order something from Lucky, and I'll get the drinks and anything else in about 15 minutes. Make a list. Relax, *jaanu*, she's just one of his girls, not the Queen of Sheba!" Then my sweet husband smiles, clears the coffee table of its heap of newspapers, magazines, and other trivia, sets the table and then leaves on his errands.

Around 6.15 pm, the doorbell rings; in an old familiar pattern which I can't quite put my finger on. I think it rather odd, that the bell should be rung when Adi has a key. By the time I get to the door, the key turns in the lock and the door opens.

My son and a sweet, smiling face, belonging to a young woman whose face and name I have never forgotten! I raise my eyebrows in enquiry, only to be met with a cool stare accompanied by a finger on the lips from Adi, fortunately standing behind her.

I give her a big hug of welcome. Questions later, I think.

My husband walks in from the bedroom and for once is speechless. For a few seconds, until he recovers his wits, smiles widely and puts out his heavy paw to her and says, "Hi Perveen, how nice to see you again after so long!"

She smiles shyly and says quietly, "It's nice to be back here, ...with Adi..." "And this time she's here to stay! I won't be stupid enough to let her go again!" booms out my son, and turns and gives her such a look of love that I get goose pimples on my arms!

A few months later, we're planning the wedding. As we sit at the dining table addressing the invitations, Adi looks up at me and says, "You know Ma, you muddled up or forgot all the other girls' names except hers. How come?"

"Mother's intuition!" I say smugly, with a big grin on my face which quickly fades into a look of panic. "Oh dear, I can't remember her parents' names," amidst howls of laughter from husband and son.

Dear reader, I would like to tell you that Perveen was like a magic potion. I started remembering names and whose faces they belonged to—now her parents want me to find a suitable young man for her sister—uh, what's her name? Umm—can't remember right now!

22

Ashtami

Manjula Shukla

It was the night of *ashtami*, the eighth day of Durga Puja. It was on this day that Goddess Durga slew Mahisasura, the buffalo demon. Mahisasura had terrorised the people and the Gods resolved to defeat him. Goddess Parvati assumed the form of Durga, the aspect of Shakti. Lord Shiva armed her with his mighty trident or *trishul*, the three pronged spear. Seated on her lion, Goddess Durga engaged in a ferocious battle with the demon and finally triumphed over him. On such nights, there is a mystical quality in the air, as if anything is possible.

It was relatively quiet on Howrah station. whice meant that instead of thousands of people thronging on the platforms, there were a few hundred.

The train moved smoothly out of the station. Bengal had come to a standstill. Business was postponed, near and dear ones had already gathered leaving only a few passengers who had to travel due to unavoidable reasons.

In a first class air-conditioned compartment for four, Mr. Soumitra Sen, for that was the name he had chosen for himself, settled himself. A tall and well built person, he looked more than his age. Deep bags under the eyes and a sizeable paunch confessed to a life of excess and debauchery. His co-passenger was listed on the chart as Devi Chowdhury aged eighteen years and the other two berths were vacant. That had looked promising and his jaded interest had perked up. The excesses of the last few days had exhausted him, the partying and the binging had been very enjoyable, but tiring. The guest list had been very impressive. Income tax officials would have given an arm and leg to know which politicians and a bureaucrats had been invited.

Sen *babu* had been celebrating. In the recent past, he had started a very lucrative venture, a matter of jubilation for his company. Just how the business was conducted was a major grey area. He had a finger in every dubious pie in the country. He had started numerous chit funds to target small investors. On maturity, his sleazy lawyers would pick out some trifling default or a late payment and confiscate the amount. The poor investors neither had the education, understanding or resources to challenge his goons and seek for recourse. Many families, already in straitened circumstances, were destroyed. They rued the day they had listened to his agents' glib assurances. And all the while, Sen *babu's* bank balance grew in geometric proportion.

As the train gathered speed, he wondered where the young girl was. Perhaps she had missed the train. Youngsters were like that these days, very careless about time and commitments. He took out the book he had picked up on the platform, a lurid paperback obtained from the book stall. A lascivious wink and a five hundred rupee note had brought it out from beneath the shelves. Sen *babu* had been born in the household of a lowly rickshaw puller and his humble origins and lack of formal education reflected in his taste for literature.

There was a timid knock and the door was partially opened to reveal a young female face. She looked younger than the eighteen years on the chart. A dusky complexion, large eyes and an attractive persona announced the arrival of Miss Devi Chowdhury.

"May I come in? I believe this is my berth" she said in a breathless voice and edged in carrying a large jute bag as her only luggage. She was dressed conservatively in a demure, pastel pink *salwar kameez* giving her a youthful appearance. Her hair was her crowning glory. A thick, long plait of gleaming, black hair touched her waist.

Sen *babu's* interest and predatory instincts were definitely aroused. "Come in, come in," he said, a little too heartily and jovially. "What happened? I thought you might have missed the train when you did not board on the platform."

"I was in the wrong compartment. It was only when the conductor *moshai* came that I realised my mistake," she said breathlessly "and I made my way to this one."

"Good, good. You are in the right place now," he said. "Be comfortable in your berth. Where are you going?"

"To Asansol. My mother gave an urgent call and I had to leave at once. Maybe Baba is not well, she wouldn't tell me. Otherwise, I would never have travelled on *ashtami*. The girls in my hostel are celebrating in a grand way. College is so much fun, specially now when such few students are left. It is holiday time you know and most of the hostelites have gone home for *Puja*. By the way, I can call you Uncle, may I?"

"Of course, you may" was the answer.

"I didn't go home for the holidays, Ma said I better stay back and study hard for the final exams, even though I think they are a long way off. I have to finish my college and get a job. We are not well off," she blushed and looked embarrassed. That was fortunate he thought, a couple of thousands would be enough to keep her happy. "Never mind, maybe I can help when the time comes," dangling such a carrot had worked wonders in the past.

"Oh, would you Uncle? It would be such a help. This ticket also must be so expensive. The travel agent must have made a mistake. I asked him for an ordinary ticket and he got an AC ticket. Ma will be upset," she said in a woebegone tone. She pulled herself together. "Look at me, I talk too much. Ma says I should learn to keep my mouth shut and be ladylike."

Sen *babu* gave a hearty laugh. "Please continue, I am enjoying your chatter. What is your name, young lady?"

"Devi," she said.

"Very appropriate, it is also the name of *Durga Ma* isn't it?" he asked.

"Yes. From childhood I have been teased about it, so much so that I even got a protector." She turned her jute bag and Sen *babu* gave a start. The face of a ferocious lion glared at him. It was so lifelike that a shiver ran down his back. There was a merry laugh. "Even you got scared Uncle. It is only a print." She got up from her seat and hung it on a peg between the two windows, the face of the lion towards them.

He looked abashed and smiled slightly, "I can see why you call it your protector."

"I call him Shera. But that's enough about me. Tell me about yourself. Who is there in your family? Where do you live? What do you do?"

Faced with such innocence, Sen *babu* felt a twinge, a remorse for his immoral thoughts. Then, as a matter of habit, he crushed his conscience.

"I am a business man. I live in Calcutta. My work is my family, that is, I am alone," he answered. He could have added that lack of family was offset by the company of innumerable pretty, young females, but that would not have been appropriate.

"Oh! How sad. It must be so awful. You must be so lonely at times," she said sympathetically. "For me, *Ma* and *Baba* are my world."

"Your parents are lucky to have you," he said.

"Now tell me what you do. You said you have a business."

"Yes, have you heard of Saraswati Finance? That is my enterprise," he said modestly.

"Oh! My goodness! I never realised, you are a very famous man. I am fortunate to have met you." Her large eyes opened even wider. She clasped her chin in her hands.

"Not at all. I am pleased to meet you. We are going to have an interesting journey together."

"Of course, but tell me something, why are you travelling by train? I would have imagined a busy person like you would have no time and would take a flight."

"The truth is that I am not comfortable in a plane. Now, do you need help to settle in?" he asked.

"Conductor *moshai* will be coming soon to check the tickets. After that I may ask you for help," she replied.

Sen *babu* looked at her with a pleased eye. Beautiful and engaging, she was a delight. She had no idea what was going on in his mind.

Conversation carried on, she prattled on in a youthful way, telling him about college life, her friends, how much she missed her parents and he kept observing her intently.

After a while there was a knock and the conductor poked his head in the doorway, "Tickets, please."

He examined the tickets offered to him and looked at the two occupants. There was some unease in his demeanour. "Shall I find you another seat? Will you be comfortable here?" he asked Devi.

"Yes, of course. Uncle is here to take care of me," she answered naively. The harassed, overworked conductor couldn't say that it was exactly what he was apprehensive about.

"Anyway, if you need me I am just outside. You can call me any time. In fact, just thump hard on the wall of the compartment, my berth is on the other side," he said and with a reassuring look, he went out.

At last, thought Sen *babu*, no one would disturb them now. He got up and locked the door. "This is the moment I have been waiting for."

"This is the moment even I have been waiting for," Sen babu gave a start of surprise. The voice had changed, it was strong and commanding. A tremor ran down his back.

He turned and looked at Devi in surprise. She smiled back, her manner as innocent as before.

"Your voice scared me," he said shakily.

"It should, that was just my voice. My form will petrify you when you see my true appearance."

Nervousness caused beads of perspiration to appear on his forehead. "What do you mean, who are you?" he cried out in fear.

"Devi."

In front of Sen *babu's* terrified eyes, she stood up, dwarfing the compartment. There was a bolt of brilliant light and Sen *babu* was blinded for a few moments. Rubbing his eyes, he got his vision back and was astounded beyond words. Her attire had changed to a golden red sari, the face and hands glittered with jewellery. Her tresses had become unbound and flowed down her back. A luminous halo encircled her head. Her entire persona was powerful and divine. The bearing was proud and fearless and the large eyes conveyed such contempt that his soul wilted with shame. The word *"Ma"* came out in strangled tones from his throat. His nostrils could catch the scent of fear.

"*Shera*" she summoned, commandingly. The ferocious lion growled menacingly in the picture and with a strong leap emerged from the jute bag and stood at her feet, snarling at him. The large, spacious compartment suddenly became claustrophobic. Sen *babu's* face turned white with terror, his knees felt weak and he fell back on his berth with fright. His heart was beating so rapidly that his entire body was quivering.

She looked at him scornfully. "Did you think that you could do anything you pleased and there would be no consequences? How many souls have you destroyed just to make yourself richer? How many crimes have you committed? How many lies have you uttered? Today is the day of payment."

He fell down on his knees. "Mercy, Ma," he whispered through dry lips.

"How does it feel to be absolutely powerless, Sen *babu?*" she said with disdain. "Did you feel any compassion for the people you cheated? Did you experience even a shred of guilt when you destroyed countless households?" There was no answer from the devastated figure in front of her.

"There is no mercy for people like you. Did you think that Gods and Goddesses were figments of people's imagination and just beautiful images to decorate calendars and the *thakur ghor*? Actually, we are the power that runs this world. Even a leaf cannot move without our permission. Today, this night of *ashtami*, your misdeeds have caught up with you. A demon like you will be slain by my hand. Prepare to go to hell." She raised her arm, the manifestation of justice and Shiva's *trishul* appeared in her hand.

Sen *Babu* cringed with terror and tried to slink under the seat. Shera growled menacingly and Devi, with a powerful movement, thrust the *trishul* straight through his heart. A blast of excruciating pain seared through his chest. The spear had entered the heart and exited from the back. The pain was rapidly spreading throughout his body. His limbs were becoming powerless. Sen *babu* looked down in horror. He was surprised that he couldn't see even a single drop of blood. He was fast losing consciousness. The last words he heard were in the innocent but panic-stricken voice of eighteen year old Devi, "Conductor *moshai*, come quickly, Sen *babu* has had a heart attack..."

23

Reveling in the Rain!

Mala Rihan

It was a sweet, drizzly day and Sudha was gazing at the drops falling on her, as she lay on the *palang* in the spacious balcony, daydreaming about the wonderful, handsome, perfect person with whom she would spend the rest of her life—once she met him of course!

"Raindrops keep falling on my head... " she hummed, as she rose to answer the door bell. It was the maid. A stocky bustling figure, she walked into the house and took a look at the chaos there.

"*Kya baby, tum ko kya ho gaya*? (Why baby, what happened to you?) Are you well?"

"I'm fine Lalitha. Just a bit tired from a hectic work week. Really feeling lazy today. Why don't we have a cup of *cha* together and then we'll both get to work?" Sudha said.

The hot sweet *cha* with a few biscuits refreshed them, and recharged, they attacked the room and began to transform it.

Sudha lived as a paying guest in a very spacious apartment overlooking the Oval. It was stylishly furnished, with an attached bath, Jacuzzi, and all gold fittings! She had been really lucky to get it when she had come from Jaipur. Her job as a design engineer in the auto industry had forced her to leave her beloved city and come here to Mumbai. When she arrived, the dirt and crowds had given her a hard time. Many nights she had cried herself to sleep and resolved to go back on the next available flight; but better sense and pride prevailed each morning.

How could she go back without earning a name and position in the industry? It had been such a struggle to get mom to agree, considering that it was the done thing in their Marwari community to marry off girls when they got out of school.

"*Bai*, just help me shift the *palang* from the balcony... Don't want to ruin it if there is a downpour tomorrow."

Sundays were busy days because the week's cleaning, shopping and beauty treatments had all to be done in that one day. Sudha's punishing daily routine left her no time on weekdays. She was out by 7.30 am to catch the 7.45 local—a truly difficult feat considering the crowds and the slippery streets. Then, an hour on, the train journey was followed by a short bus or rickshaw ride and she would be in time for office at nine. Of course "many a slip" occasionally led to being JIT (just in time) which basically meant before the boss landed in! He was frequently late too because he was coming in from the other direction—from Kandivali which was the direction in which most commuters were traveling.

For Sudha this Sunday was one such busy day. No different. She was cleaning, washing and stocking up for the week to come. She had also promised herself a couple of hours at the beauty parlor for a pampering facial and other essentials. The loud jangle of the front door bell suddenly interrupted her thoughts. Where was everybody? Her landlady Ruby had a devoted Man Friday who looked after both, the house and his mistress, with great precision. Maybe it was his day off!

She put down her load of clothes and continued her instructions to her maid, "*Yeh kapade dhone hai. Aur dekh ke, laal wale ka rang jaata hai.*" (The clothes are to be washed. And careful, the red one will bleed.)

She made her way through the richly furnished drawing room to the front door, as the bell clanged once again. "Coming!" she shouted as she reached for the door knob.

An impatient looking youngish man stood outside. She timidly asked whom he had come to meet, but he lost no time in answering her query and walked in, bags and all, straight to the drawing room.

Bahadur, the Man Friday, made his appearance and very quickly took charge. She could hear his placatory "But Pratapji we didn't have any idea, otherwise the car would have been there at the airport to receive you!"

Sudha returned to the sanctuary of her room. As she shut the door behind her, a long arm yanked it open again, and a slightly stern looking Pratapji strode in! She froze! His dark brown eyes raked the room, taking in the undies strewn over a chair and the *palang* lying across, having been abandoned half way while she had run to get the door.

She could feel defensive words rising to her lips, when Bahadur came to the rescue. "Pratapji, we have put you in the green guest room. Sudhaji is staying in this one."

Ruby walked in to add to the confusion… her loud "Oh Pratap! How wonderful to see you!" was followed by a big hug, to which Pratap bent enough to envelope his short, rotund but affectionate aunt.

A curt "Sorry" emerged from Pratap's lips as Ruby went into details of who Sudha was and how she came to be occupying his room. Closing the door behind them, Sudha stood surveying the disastrous condition of her room. She chuckled to herself!

All rules of no washing, no foodstuff etc., were obviously not being obeyed. Thank God, Ruby had been so caught up in Pratap that hopefully she hadn't noticed!

Doing a quick sweep of all the contraband and heaving it into the cupboard, Sudha hurried for the facial.

Dinner time brought formal introductions to the guest, Ruby's sister's son Pratap Mahajan, who had just flown in from London and would be leaving for Delhi in a day or so. Ruby proudly told her that her nephew was a business man always on the move. Singapore, London, Dubai and South Africa, he had interests in many parts of the world. Now, a relaxed Pratap smiled and looked at his aunt indulgently, no doubt used to her taking pride in his activities.

"I've brought you a new toy, Ruby. Maybe Sudha will help you get used to it." Pratap glanced at Sudha.

Out came an iPad encased in a handsome leather cover. Ruby squealed, "You shouldn't have!" But she was obviously thrilled! Pratap patiently began teaching her how to use it.

Sudha looked on for a bit and then retired to her room. Dreams of a handsome young man kept her enthralled till she awoke the next morning to the sound of the alarm. Blushing at the trend of her thoughts, she jumped from her bed. The weekend had been good, now back to the daily grind!

During the course of the week, Bahadur seemed extra busy, but there was little sign of the nephew. Ruby let it drop that Pratap had left for Singapore, but would be back over the weekend. Sudha found her thoughts weaving around the young Pratap's life. She casually asked a few details from Bahadur, who was only too happy to let her know that after a broken engagement last year, Pratap was unattached.

Her weekly call to mom carefully edited out any mention of this chance meeting. Knowing mom, she would be only too happy, but also quick to jump to conclusions. 'There's nothing like that. He's only my land lady's nephew! Why mention it?'

Yet her heart missed a beat whenever his name was mentioned. She had taken to coming home early to sit with Ruby and her iPad, showing her how to make a Facebook account, play games etc. The young, recently widowed Ruby was fun, she had a wry sense of humor and was never at a loss for words. She had no children of her own, so took a great interest in all her nephews and nieces. Pratap was the eldest and a great favorite. After his uncle' s untimely death, he had made it a point to stop at Mumbai whenever possible, showering his aunt with gifts and taking her out for plays and movies or just for dinner to the Taj.

As luck would have it, the monsoons made a sudden comeback and rains lashed the city on Friday. She had an important meeting and took the 7:45 train, praying and hoping that she would reach safely. The rain continued unabated and reports began filtering in about the flooding of roads and of tracks. Her colleagues advised her not to return home, and they all decided to stay the night in the office, stocking up on tea, *Samosas*, bun *maska* and cream rolls from the local Irani store. The owner had kindly kept his shop open for all those who needed shelter.

Water swirled around the steps and was at least one-and-a-half feet deep. Several cars lay abandoned on the roads, and there were groups of people, bravely forming chains to navigate the flooded roads. Many walked miles to get home only to find homes flooded or inaccessible. Calling Ruby to inform her, Sudha was struck by the warm concern in her voice. "It is safer for you to stay there my dear. The TV reports that there is extensive flooding and trains are unlikely to reach."

Chatting and nibbling with friends, time flew and they nodded off with the lights on, sitting on the thick carpets, wrapped in *dupattas* and shawls. In the morning, they washed and ventured down to assess the situation. The water level appeared the same, perhaps it had gone down a couple of inches, but traveling was out of the question for those dependent on public transport.

With bun *maskas* washed down with a hot *cuppa*, they waded back to the office and rolled down their apparel. Working was their only entertainment, apart from the news caught on laptops occasionally. Phone lines and even mobiles worked only intermittently. Mid morning, Sudha found her cell ringing... it was dear Ruby, checking on her!

"Good morning Ruby, how's the rain treating you?"

"Sudha my dear, I am so worried about you. Listen. Pratap's landed at the airport last night and has been stuck there since then. I have got hold of a Sumo to pick him from there. They will come to your office as soon as they can... It is on the way, so don't worry. Please come home with them!"

So sweet and thoughtful of Ruby! Grateful to her, Sudha settled down to wait, hoping they would make it home today.

After a couple of hours, there was a loud knock and a uniformed chauffeur entered asking for Sudha madam. Gladly she went down, after hugging the few who would have to spend yet another night at the office.

Pratap was sitting inside, looking as businesslike as ever. As she entered the car, he smiled and she most irrationally, began feeling as if he was a knight rescuing her.

"Wet enough for you?" His smile was now really charming and infectious.

Sudha managed a weak smile, and said "I always love the rain, but this time it's a deluge!"

It was a long way home, but time flew as the two chatted away like old friends.

A hot shower and soup later, they were sitting for dinner. Sudha was quiet, listening to Pratap regaling his Aunt with details of his trip... and their ride from the airport.

Ruby had laid out a big spread, and they sat together in the warm dining room, sipping some brandy to take away the chill. Laughing and chatting, they let go of the day's events.

From then on, for Sudha the weeks just flew by, what with work and travel and weekend trysts with Pratap. They had become good friends and had begun to look forward to being with each other.

Like all ladies of her generation, Ruby was a matchmaker at heart. She broached the topic with Pratap and meeting little resistance, realized that the two were indeed interested in each other. But the broken engagement had made Pratap cautious about commitment.

He would require some persuasion, as would Sudha, but Ruby was confident of success!

24

Not This Time, You Don't!

Jayashree Dhillon

The phone rang shrilly, disturbing her concentration. Priya was working on her research paper. She had forgotten to keep her cell phone on silent mode. About to cut the call, her eyes fell on the caller's name on the mobile's screen. Her heart skipped a beat. It was Rajeev. Rajeev Khanna, her college friend. Dashing, suave and handsome Rajeev. An impossible flirt. Every girl had a soft corner for him. He had the knack of making each one of them feel special. She answered the phone a little breathlessly. Rajeev always had that effect on her.

"Hello gorgeous! How are you? I'm in your city for just a couple of hours. Business trip. Meet me for lunch. I'm starving and I'm not taking 'no' for an answer," said Rajeev in his rich voice.

So typical, thought Priya. That was Rajeev. No news, no calls. Not even an e-mail… for ages. Then suddenly he would materialise and put her life in a spin. Priya's heart was beating fast. With an approaching deadline, the last thing she needed was a distraction of this kind.

It was always like this. Priya and Rajeev had been classmates in college. They were good friends and very close to each other.

Priya always had a crush on him. She suspected even he knew that. But in spite of his compliments, his flirtatious ways, he seemed more like a buddy to her. He would confide in her, about his escapades, even his heart breaks… with other women. "Priya, you are special. You are my best friend. The only one who can understand me," Rajeev would gush.

Priya remembered that first time. Rajeev was really broken after his affair with Tanya—another classmate. Just two hours before the last Economics paper in their final exams, he phoned Priya and shouted, "I'm not appearing for the paper. I can't. After all those promises of undying love and a life together, Tanya has gone and got engaged to a rich businessman from Dubai. He is ten years older than her, for God's sake! I am finished."

Priya reasoned with him for the next half an hour, calmed him down and said, "We will talk about this after the paper. Now, I want you to pick up your hall ticket, ID card and come to college."

"I'm only doing it for you," said Rajeev, his voice trailing off. It was to Priya's credit that Rajeev not only appeared for the paper but also managed to do it quite well. After the paper, in the college canteen, several coffees and cigarettes later, Rajeev held Priya's hand, gave her his famous 'little boy lost' smile and said, "What will I do without you, Sweets? Thank you for being there for me." Priya couldn't contain her happiness. But that was that. Nothing more.

Another time, just after college, when most of them were struggling to get a decent job, Rajeev dropped in at her department at the University. "I am so worried, Priya. My father has had a heart attack. He is in the ICU. I feel as if it's all my fault. I refused to join his business and started working in an ad agency. The shock must have been too much for him that his only son, did not want to join the family business."

Later that evening, Rajeev took Priya for a drive 'to get away from the gloomy atmosphere of the hospital.' He pulled over to the side of the road and actually wept on Priya's shoulders saying, "I hope he will be fine, Priya. Please pray for him."

"Of course I will, Rajeev. I am sure your dad will be fine soon," replied Priya.

***

A couple of years later, Priya was attending a conference in Paris. She stood, a tiny figure in front of the Eiffel Tower, awe-struck by its magnificence. A familiar voice broke into her reverie. "Surprises shall never cease! Look who is here? My very own dear friend Priya!" Priya was astounded. Fancy meeting Rajeev in Paris. She was in a state of shock. Rajeev's happiness at this chance meeting was obvious. He gave Priya a big hug and said, "Stop looking as if you have seen a ghost. Aren't you happy to see me? I most certainly am. I am here for a hoteliers' convention. By the way, I have joined my father's business. C'mon now, I am going to show you around Paris. It is the most beautiful city in the world. A city for lovers."

The next two days Priya was in a daze, soaking in the sights of Paris. The leisurely walks by the Seine, the coffee and croissants in way side cafes, the treasure trove of art at the Louvre and the shopping in fashionable shops. Rajeev was at his charming best and Priya loved every moment of his attention.

Seeing her off at the airport, Rajeev said with feeling, "It's just been so wonderful here in Paris with you. I'll always treasure these moments." Then with a lingering hug and a voice gruff with emotion, he said, "Bye, Priya. Take care. See you sometime." Then, he flashed her a dazzling smile and with a wave of his hand, he disappeared into the crowds.

Sitting inside the plane, waiting for take-off, Priya was lost in her thoughts. 'What could one make of Rajeev? So friendly, so warm, so affectionate–while he was with her. But once he left, there was no communication from him at all. No keeping in touch. Maybe, there was a woman in his life. He always had a woman in his life. But she was his friend, so how come he didn't tell her anything about his lady love? What about her? God knows, she found Rajeev very attractive and she was always a bit annoyed at her own reaction to his sudden visits and equally sudden disappearing acts. Why did it upset her? Was this love? No, it couldn't be.' Whenever he left, after a day or two of being out of sorts, Priya always settled into her routine. She didn't think about him, nor did she miss him.

***

"Excuse me, is this your hand bag?" Priya snapped out of her day dreaming to look into the brown eyes of a fellow passenger.

"Oh yes! Sorry." She picked up her bag so that the man could sit down on the empty seat beside her. Soon the two of them were chatting like old friends. His name was Ravi Krishnaswamy. His friends called him Krish. He worked for Microsoft in Bangalore. He was returning from a business meeting followed by a holiday in the wine growing areas of France. They had similar interests—books, music, theatre and travel. By the time the plane touched down at Bangalore airport, they had exchanged phone numbers, e-mail ids and each other's addresses. They said their good-byes at the airport.

"I'll call you," said Krish, as a parting shot. Priya nodded, smiled and pushed her trolley towards the waiting cab. She had barely got out of the airport, when her mobile phone rang. It was Krish. "Hey, I was thinking, how about dinner tomorrow?"

'So soon?' Priya thought to herself, smiled and agreed.

"I can pick you up around eight, after work. It will give me a chance to meet your parents too," said Krish, happy that she had accepted his invitation.

Things worked out well after that. Priya's parents liked Krish. Even her stern father approved of the intelligent, down-to-earth and unassuming young man. Several meetings followed. Krish and Priya were spending more and more time together. Priya's mother, a simple, traditional lady, often invited Krish over for family dinners, especially on festivals. Her parents were secretly hoping that Priya would settle down with Krish.

Krish too, had made it pretty obvious that he cared for Priya immensely. It was Priya who was not sure about taking this relationship forward. Oh yes, she cared for him deeply! Krish was all that a woman could ask for from a partner. He was mature, caring, steady and dependable. Always there for her. In fact, perfect husband material! But she had to confront the truth – what if Rajeev popped up again into her life? Fun loving, exciting Rajeev. There wasn't a dull moment when he was around.

A year went by. Then one afternoon, Priya's phone rang while she was at work. It was Rajeev. "Hi sweetheart! I am here in your city again. Just dying to see you. How about dinner? You name the place. I'll pick you up and we can go dancing afterwards."

Just briefly, Priya was at a loss for words as mixed emotions swept through her. She was excited to hear Rajeev's voice on the phone but she was upset that as always he had burst into her life without warning and expected her to drop everything to be with him.

"Priya are you still there?" Rajeev interrupted her thoughts.

At that moment, Priya made up her mind. She said in a calm voice, "Of course Rajeev, it will be lovely to meet you. Come home. Krish is picking me up at eight thirty tonight. The three of us can go down to the club for drinks and dinner."

A pregnant silence followed. "Who is Krish? You never told me about him. You got married?" accused Rajeev.

"Not yet," replied Priya smiling to herself. "But do come, I am sure Krish would love to meet you."

As Priya put down the receiver, she thought to herself, 'You don't upset me anymore. No, Rajeev! Not this time, you don't!'

❏ ❏ ❏

25

A Tribute to ISA

Manjula Shukla

Life was not fair, why was she suffering so much in her old age? Zohrabi's old, tired eyes were red from weeping. She had cried so much no tears were left. 'A thousand curses on the *Badshah's* head. May he know no peace, may his entire family be wiped out, no one left even to mourn for the dead.' Even her throat could not say a word, it was parched and aching. She had not swallowed a morsel of food or a gulp of water since the terrible news had hit her on the head.

It seemed just yesterday that her beloved son, Isa, had been a toddler, picking himself up from the ground after a few faltering steps. How her heart had burst with happiness to see him. This was in the olden times when her husband had been alive, God rest his soul in peace. The evil eye had cast a malevolent look and he had succumbed to small pox. Overnight life had changed forever. His business partners vanished with all the money and Zohrabi and Isa were literally on the streets. At times, she felt so despondent that she felt like ending her life but the thought of Isa, somehow, kept her going. She had to take care of him. Life had been a tough struggle and making ends meet, a Herculean task. She had worked day and night in other people's homes, cleaning, cooking, stitching and mending, trying to earn an honest living.

The next day that stood out in her memory was the one when Isa, just a small child, had constructed a model of a palace from a few bricks he had found on the roadside. "*Ammi*, this is what I'm going to do" he had announced with such joy and exhilaration that it seemed as if the sun was shining out of his eyes. She had looked at him, heart bursting with love and pride.

As soon as he could, Isa got a job on a construction site. Though he was probably the youngest worker, he put his heart and soul into the work. At that tender age, he attracted the attention of the *Badshah's* chief architect and the nobles. He would make a small change in design, tiny enough to be of no consequence, but the stones in the building sang their song. Whatever he touched acquired, an intangible quality that spoke volumes.

Zohrabi's heart still ached when she recalled how he used to come home, worn out after a hard day's work, back aching and limbs tired beyond exhaustion. Yet but his face shone with happiness because he enjoyed his work so much. It was not work, it was passion. In fact it was his life itself.

In spite of the sadness burdening her mind, her face creased in a faint smile. Accolades had poured in for her son's achievements. The emperor had, himself, gifted him a purse of gold when he had successfully completed the prestigious fort. Then after the death of the Empress, a massive project had been announced. The architects had been chosen. Ustad Ahmed Lahori had been given the responsibility of creating poetry in marble and Khan, his right hand, was entrusted with the task of seeing it come alive.

Years had passed. There had been times when Isa had not come home for days on end. Then Zohrabi would packed his meals and walk the distance to where the construction was being done, on the banks of the river Yamuna. Sometimes she was able to meet him. At other times, he would be up on the scaffolding busy directing the labourers. Then she would quietly look away, afraid of disturbing him when he was so far away from the ground. The workers adored him. He was never too arrogant to speak politely to the menial labourers, never too tired to lend a sympathetic ear to their woes and never too uncaring to show concern for their well-being. They could sense his magic touch. His drive and love for the building inspired them to do their best. The construction was par excellence, not out of fear of the *Badshah*, but out of love for Isa.

So many times Zohrabi had talked to him about marrying and settling down. He would laugh and change the topic. In their tradition, the proposal was sent by the groom's family. In the case of Isa, interested noblemen trooped to Zohrabi with proposals of their beautiful and talented daughters. Isa would brush them aside. When Zohrabi threatened to go on a fast unto death, he relented but said that he would take a decision only after the completion of the project. Did he have an intuition of the situation to come? Maybe.

Finally the tomb was completed, an achievement which was unparalleled in the history of the world, the Taj Mahal. The workers were jubilant, the engineers' and architects' joy knew no bounds. The emperor had been very pleased, but how had he shown his pleasure?

"Open the door, *Apa*, open the door," Parveen, Zohrabi's neighbour hammered urgently on the front door in the middle of the night.

"What's the matter, is this the time to disturb anyone?" Zohrabi got up with difficulty, her joints were acting up. She opened the door and saw stark fear in Parveen's eyes.

"*Apa*, rumour has it that the *Badshah* is blinding the workers and cutting off their hands."

"Allah be merciful, why?"

"They are saying that the workers should never be able to create anything as beautiful as the Taj."

Zohrabi's heart stood still. "Isa, Isa," she screamed like a mad woman, rushing from room to room, "where are you?"

Isa was rudely awakened from his death like slumber, earned after years of unceasing toil. "*Ammi*," he said, rubbing his eyes, "what's happened?"

"Listen to what Parveen is saying" she narrated the rumour punctuated with heartrending sobs.

Isa straightened his back with a resigned look. "Actually *Ammi*, I have been expecting this and I am prepared. I have seen the true nature of the *Badshah* and anyway my life's ambition is achieved. No other building will ever be as beautiful, in any corner of this *jahan*. It is mine, it may belong to the *Badshah*, but it is mine. I built it with my hands, my sweat and blood. Today I am going to leave my personal mark on it, such a mark that no one will ever be able to erase it. It will be a beauty spot like a *chand ka dhabba*. I am going out now, but don't worry, I'll be back."

That was when Zohrabi's tears started flowing. Every second was like eternity until she heard his footsteps returning. She clutched him as if she was drowning, which she was, in a pool of fear. "Isa, my *jaan*, why don't we leave this instant, go far away where no one knows us, away from the cruel *Badshah*?" she pleaded.

"Hush *Ammi*, I refuse to run away like a scared rat. Let the *Badshah* do his worst, I am ready for it. I have left my signature and it will be seen for all time to come. Come *Ammi*, be proud of your son." He hugged her tightly and together they sat the whole night, she resting her weary head on his strong shoulder.

Soon enough there was the dreaded knock on the door. Officers of the *Badshah's* elite force, the *Fauj-i-hind* stood outside. "The Badshah has summoned Isa Khan," they said stone faced.

Isa hugged his mother for the last time and with proud, erect shoulders walked out with his mother's wail ringing in his ears "Isa, don't go, I can't live without you."

Later that day, a gentle breeze wafted Isa's last thought *'Ammi'* towards his home but it fell on deaf ears. Zohrabi had spoken the truth, she couldn't live without Isa.

Every year during the monsoon there is a steady drip of rain water inside the main hall of the Taj Mahal, a poignant reminder of the anguish suffered by the workers and their families. Though centuries have passed, no one till date has been able to figure out where Isa Khan made a tiny leak in the dome.

It also seemed that Zohrabi's curses did indeed bring about the downfall of the mighty Mughal Empire. There was much infighting among the heirs to the throne after the reign of Shah Jahan. Aurangzeb ascended the throne after having his elder brother Dara Shikoh killed. He was the last noteworthy ruler of the Mughal Empire.

❑ ❑ ❑

26

Pinki Learns to Say "No!"

Mala Rihan

It was a dreary and cold day in December. Winter in Delhi could be very dismal. The sun had barely shown its face for the past three days. Clouds and the haze had combined to screen the sunlight and the result was truly depressing. Even the boys didn't want to go out and play cricket as they would normally. Holidays meant that the house was crawling with people; relatives from all small towns congregated in Delhi, leaving it to the local residents to make necessary arrangements for their comfortable stay, and of course, food and entertainment. This made the young ones very happy, but the women of the house were at the mercy of the elements, and their hired help.

"Bibiji!" It was the dhobi from the corner *thela* (cart). Pinki's mother, Lalita motioned him to the room where the clothes were stashed, neatly segregated into piles for ironing and washing. As she seated herself and gave herself into the soothing routine, she was able to appreciate the clockwork efficiency with which all these helpers came and went, leaving her with only minimal supervisory tasks. Even that kept her busy–handling such a large household was a skill she had been trained for, from the day she married.

Today was Wednesday and it was just the beginning of the winter break. Her brother's family of four was here together with her cousin's kids from Meerut. *Badi Mamiji*, her husband's aunt, was expected any time now–she had left from Panipat in the morning, but was caught in a traffic jam within Delhi.

Her own daughter Pinki was just five but a bit of a mouse, always trying to stick to her mother. Really, Montu should take better care of his kid sister. A ten year old with an immense amount of energy, he was normally in the park playing with a rowdy group of friends of all ages and sizes. He would never take Pinki along. And if she insisted, would abandon her at any other park while he buzzed off to play with his friends. A sobbing Pinki would straggle back to the house to sit with *Amma,* the elderly household help. *Amma* was only too happy to set aside her daily humdrum chores to entertain the little girl, telling her stories from her own village, thus distracting her from the feeling of rejection and hurt.

"*Ramu! Kithe mar gaya tu?*" (Ramu! where are you?) It was her mother-in-law shouting for the young servant boy or *mundu*. He was only twelve and had no idea of house work. Whenever he got the chance, he'd run off to the terrace or hide in his room. He was passionately fond of water, so any task involving the use of copious amounts of water was assigned to him…watering the lawn, or washing the terrace.

Time to check on lunch, she couldn't forget the *dahi wadas* that *mamiji* loved. The thick sweet tamarind and *gur chutney* was ready, but the little fried urad dal dumplings had to be soaked in warm water, then put into the whipped curds, seasoned just right with salt, sugar, zeera powder and green coriander leaves, something that she had to attend to personally. This ensured that her *dahiwadas* were the softest and most delicious.

"What's the secret ingredient, Lalita?" her friends would ask. She would just give a quiet smile of satisfaction and insist they have some more.

At last it was all done, and it was time to get ready. She pushed open the bathroom door to give herself a relaxing facial scrub before lunch.

"*Arre!* What is the matter, Pinki?" she exclaimed. Her little daughter was sitting perched on the pot with tears streaming down her cheeks.

"Let me see what is wrong. Come with me, baby." Saying this, she lifted the crying child and brought her to the bed.

Her mind was racing through the possibilities... 'was Pinki constipated? Or had the *chaat* last evening been too spicy? Whatever was wrong?' When asked, all the child would say was that it was paining. She was having pain while passing urine. A quick call and Dr. Banoo, her trusted pediatrician and friend, rushed over to examine the whimpering child.

"*He Bhagwan!* Your daughter seems to have acquired a vaginal infection. However did that happen?"

Dr. Banoo gave her friend a meaningful look, so as to say, we'll talk about it, but not in front of the child. She spoke to Pinki very kindly, applied a soothing salve, and treatment was begun immediately. Soon Pinki's pain subsided. But the question about where and how she had picked up the infection remained unanswered. Every query by her mother or the doctor was answered by a flood of tears. And there were so many people in the house. Someone might overhear. What shame it would bring to the *khandan*.

Only Pinki knew how she had got the pain. And she was not telling. Because they had told her that the grownups would beat her if she told. And they would throw her out on the streets, she would become a beggar.

"They" were omnipotent and omnipresent. "They" would come after her again with sweet words, chocolates and promises of stories. She thought of the pain and her mother's tears. Mummy kept asking her who had "touched" her, but seeing her little face break into tears, eventually stopped. She finally gave up. But she did make sure that Pinki was not left alone. Montu, to his great disgust, was given the task of escorting her to the playground. A maid was deputed to keep an eye on her and keep her safe.

But "they" were not far. And "they" were on the lookout for the time that she would be found alone.

Sure enough, one day the young maid complained of stomach pain, and took off to her room for the afternoon. Montu's friends were playing carrom in the playroom. Pinki hung around her mother, holding on to an edge of her sari, till exasperated, Lalita told her to go and sleep in her room for a while. She felt safe in Mummy's room. She lay down on the bed under the thick *rajai* and closed her eyes.

She didn't even hear them, they came so quietly. Their hands searched under the *rajai* and began the touching. She cowered inside, hoping they would go away. That the maid would come. That Mummy would call. She lay frozen, thinking that if she didn't move they might go away.

The elder one pulled the *rajai* from her face. Alarmed, her eyes popped open.

"Oh you're awake! You were pretending to sleep, huh? Come on let's play. See we brought chocolate for you. And I have a new story about the Prince and Princess for you."

"No," said Pinki, very softly as though to herself. Then she said it louder, "No!"

"Don't you want to play with us? Here's the chocolate." It was a large Cadbury's Fruit and Nut. But she had said no. And they were listening to her. Feeling more confident, she said it again, very loudly. "NO!"

This time her voice carried and the boys were afraid they might be caught. They ran quickly back to the carrom board. And put on their most innocent expressions, and began a mock fight to establish their presence there. The alert Lalita had heard some sounds, and came running to her room from the guest room where she had been chatting with *Badi Mamiji*.

She found Pinki sitting up on the bed confidently. "I said NO, Mummy!" She exclaimed. A shiver ran down Lalita's spine. Her blood ran cold as she realized what her five-year-old, her sweet innocent daughter had said. She picked her up saying, *"Bahut acha kiya beti!"* and holding her tight, wept for her darling's lost innocence. For her own limitations, for the nature of the strange world we live in, where safety is so ephemeral.

***

A pregnant Pinki stared down at her daughter, a five-year-old, used to constant taunts because of being born a girl. Her sonography had shown that her second child was also a girl, and the demands for termination of the pregnancy were still ringing in her ears. She realized it was time to say no again. She would say "No!" to the abusive alcoholic husband and "No!" to the demands of her in laws. She and her daughters could live by themselves, and this time she was old enough and sensible enough to know that her brother Montu and her loving parents would always be there to support her.

❏ ❏ ❏

27

Bridal Bedlam

Rita Chhablani

It is a family wedding; the bride is her niece, a girl at whose birth, Rina had been present. The momentum builds up as the D-day draws closer. Excitement surges through her.

What to wear is the eternal question, most perplexing to all of womankind. Vacant-eyed, Rina stares into her wardrobe spilling over with clothes, as though she is seeing them for the first time. Trying on a multitude of sari blouses of varied hues, she flings them aside in frustration, since most of them are bursting at the seams. The words of a song from the movie *Chandni*, featuring the voluptuous Sridevi, come floating to her mind... *"kal choli silaayi thi aaj tung ho gayi..."* (yesterday I had a blouse tailored, today it has become tight already). But she is no Sridevi, she realises, and flops down angrily on her bed.

Maybe a new sari will do the trick? Yes, that indeed may be the easiest solution to the current dilemma. Besides, the blouse will be made to her present measurements. Perfect. She is proud of herself.

The purposeful look in her eyes, as she strides into the living room, does not go unnoticed by her husband, who conveniently hides his face behind the newspaper. She knows him too well, so she snatches the paper from his hands. Settling down beside him on the sofa, she says with a pout, "I have nothing to wear for my cousin's daughter's wedding!"

"My poor, little, rich wife," he clucks his tongue with utmost sympathy.

"You are making fun of me," she complains.

"Come to the point, how much do you want?" he asks.

Mission accomplished, Rina's face lights up. She squeals with delight. "How did you know? You are truly omniscient. That is why I love you so much."

Sharad rolls his eyes. Women! Know one, know them all. There must be some of exceptions, of course.

Not his wife, though!

***

Mumbai

Rina arrives at the guest house with a mountain of bags and feels as if she has been sucked into a whirlwind. Weddings are exhilarating, sheer fun and enjoyment at somebody else's expense. She would certainly not like to be in the shoes of Ashok, the bride's father, her dear cousin's husband, however. Expectations run high. So do tempers.

She spots Ashok. He sees her too and his face lights up and he waves. She rushes towards him and says, "Hi," giving him a big hug. She is his *saali*, his wife's sister, his favourite and rightfully, as the saying goes, his *aadhi gharwaali*. Half his wife!

"Can I help?" she asks. She does want to, sincerely. The phone rings and he, pats her shoulder in thanks and walks away, heading to the area where peace and quiet reign—the terrace.

The poor fellow, she thinks. He is required to wave a magic

wand and find miraculous solutions to complex problems. And that too without losing his calm. She watches him silently. He is constantly besieged with calls, one after the other. Rina is sure these must be never-ending queries from the bridal party or a constant stream of calls from the groom's side of the family.

Pressure is mounting. She admires him, though. He is calmness personified. Not a furrow on his forehead. A "cool guy." as his college-going sons would say. She had known of this quality from the day he had married her pampered cousin, some twenty odd year ago.

Rina sees Ashok's mother and heads towards the matriarch of the family, who is where she is expected to be, by the dining table, wolfing down forbidden food like samosas and potato *tikkis* because she thinks no one is looking.

Rina settles her tired body into the vacant dining chair beside her. "Your son deserves a gold medal," she says to the older woman, then stares at the delicacies, holds back, gives in at once and is totally ready to dive into the delicious food tempting her. She pours generous helpings of the yummy Sindhi curry into a bowl, piles it with rice, tops it with the sinfully sweet *boondi*. A few potato *tikkis*, the piquant green chutney, doesn't do anyone any harm, besides, they complete the deal. By now, all her five senses are screaming and with utmost delight she digs in and takes her first bite. *If there is heaven it is this, it is this, it is this...* she thinks of the famous poet who had said some such words about Kashmir. He had probably not eaten fare such as this!

Silence, as she finishes the sinful fare. The waist can go to waste, for all she cares now.

She looks around for Ashok. Has he eaten? He is no longer visible. He must have left on one of the multifarious last minute errands that crop up despite months of planning and long lists.

Food coma takes over now. She gets up in search of the nearest empty bed. Unfortunately, with a house as full as this, a guesstimate of at least thirty, she soon discovers that all the beds are taken.

A multitude of 'Aunties' and 'Uncles' lie sprawled in peaceful slumber in every room, their booming snores reverberating. Nothing shatters her coma-like state however. It is the insidious magic of the Sindhi curry and rice at work. In her haze, she makes a compromise and heads for the sofa, but it is house full there too. Long lost cousins and friends are sprawled across it, chatting and giggling, intent on catching up.

"Hi," says one, a second cousin, on seeing her. "Join us." She moves over and Rina settles down. One should thank God for such mercies in difficult times such as these.

Despite her zombie-like state, she cannot help overhearing snippets of juicy conversation.

"Your daughter has grown so big," comments an elderly aunt to a younger lady beside her, who has a daughter well past the acceptable marriageable age.

'Ouch, that hurt!' Rina feels like slapping her father's distant cousin for this innuendo, which she thinks is subtle but is so insensitive.

"Can you suggest a good boy, educated but who will not ask for much dowry?" begs the other, saying the last bit, hesitatingly.

Rina cannot help shooting out, "Why do mothers of daughters have to demean themselves so? Such hypocrisy!"

The aunt and the lady both glare at her as if to ask, "Who asked you for your advice?"

Rina gets the message. Silence is golden at times such as these and she shuts her eyes.

"*Bewakoof!* Stupid!" Her antenna picks up a vituperative whisper and she is alert in a moment. "You can never do anything right, can you?" It sounds like a familiar voice. She cannot help opening her eyes and eavesdropping shamelessly. It is her cousin, Rakesh's wife glowering at him.

The family has always pitied him. His wife bullies him behind closed doors, spurs him into action, while she sits around looking at everyone helplessly as he goes into a wild rage in public. Does the woman think we all are fools? The family knows the games she plays.

"Rina, the food was too spicy," a US-based distant aunt's daughter complains in her pseudo accent. "I hardly ate."

Liar, Rina feels like saying, having seen the complainant return for second and third helpings. She opens her mouth to retort but better sense tells her to conserve her energy for more important things.

A sweat-drenched Ashok, looking quite harassed, suddenly walks in. Clapping his hands, he tries to catch everyone's attention. "Come on, come on, I have an important announcement to make," he says.

"There are no towels in this flat, or what?" asks an aunt hurrying towards him.

"Shh," says Rina angrily. "Wait, I will go find some for you."

"The cook has a list! He wants dry fruits, saffron and the milk has curdled," the aunt in charge of the kitchen appears out of nowhere, looking very harassed.

"Why don't you call the grocer and ask him to deliver the things," suggests the poor man calmly.

"Uncle is there an ironing man close by?" asks the girl with the accent.

"Uncle, the Bisleri water bottles are over."

"We need a car for our appointment at the beauty parlour," pipe in two stylish young women.

Rina feels sorry for the man, who seemed to have forgotten the important announcement he had come to make. He stands looking perplexed and stares around him blankly. He finally flings his arms up in the air in exasperation, turns to go away when he remembers, for he turns around and says, "All I came here to say is that the two *mehndiwalis* will be here soon. So, you, Rina, will you take charge, please?"

"Of course, I will boss," she says, hoping he would smile as he usually does. But this time there is no reaction, instead, once again he is on the phone, stuck to his ear.

Within half an hour, the two professional young women arrive, carrying their paraphernalia. This is a time for fun; getting your hands hennaed. It gives a feeling of joy, heralding the wedding. There is a sudden commotion, each rushing to the *mehndiwalis* with extended hands.

"Me first," the young women and girls scream, pushing aside the elderly aunts who are slowly limping along.

A happy chatter fills the air. Rina is in no hurry. Her head is throbbing by now. She can feel her migraine acting up. She needs the cup that cheers! A quick call to her cousin to find out if all is well and everything under control and she makes her way to the kitchen.

The head cook sits on a stool like a monarch of all he surveys, busy directing his subordinates who are vigorously stirring simmering gravies in various pots.

"*Maharaj*, can I have a cup of tea, please?" she requests in a voice dripping with honey. "No one makes it like you," she adds as a punch line to boost the man's ego.

A short while later, a cool breeze fans her face, feet up on a chair, she sits on the huge terrace. It is her moment of quiet and she gratefully sips the super-strong, super-sweet, ginger-laced tea and munches on some of the *sattas,* the homemade yummy cookies the chef very graciously has given.

Within a couple of hours, she hears people making a mad rush for the bathrooms. The fittest, the very agile, and the most aggressive make it to the winning post! Voices shout for safety pins, hair pins and help with sari pleats.

In the middle of all this, arrives the bride. Rina looks at her tenderly. She remembers being present at her birth. Now the baby is almost a woman and about to be married. She goes in, hugs her and plants a big kiss on her fair cheek.

"Aunty, I just came here straight from the beauty parlour, you know waxing and all," says Chandni, her niece, who is looking anything but radiant.

Rina takes charge. Getting the most comfortable chair vacated for the bride, she seats her and rushes to the kitchen to fetch her a cup of coffee and some snacks. She is sure her niece has not eaten anything.

"No, I am too nervous, not hungry, Rina aunty," protests Chandni.

Somehow Rina cajoles her into having a few sips of the hot liquid and some bites of the delectable *Maharaj*-made cashew brittle. This chef is a class apart.

The bridal ceremonies begin in full earnest with the girl painting Chandni's palms and hands with pretty designs.

"Poor girl, she does look so exhausted," Rina calls and says to her cousin, a short while later. "You should see how she keeps looking longingly at the bed."

"Why don't you try getting her to sleep for some time?" her cousin suggests.

Rina tries but does not succeed. The girl is too keyed up. She says, "You know, Rina aunty, I have not been sleeping for the last couple of days. I am too tired to even dream of my Prince Charming, the knight with whom I am going to spend my entire life."

Or seven lives, if folklore is to be believed, Rina thinks. Why are weddings so stressful for the bride, she wonders.

"Wait for a second, will you Chandni?" she says to her niece. "I will accompany you downstairs to your car and see you off."

Five minutes later, Rina rushes down to find the car missing. Her niece is gone. Shrugging her shoulders she makes her way back up, finds that the *mehndiwali* is free. She gets a mere dot as *shagun* put on one of her hands and goes back to sit on the terrace.

The shrill ring of her mobile shatters her peaceful moments of reprieve. It is her cousin sister. "Is Chandni there? I want to ask her something," she says. "I can't get hold of my dear husband, as usual. Just when I need him."

"Chandni left a short while ago," Rina responds and hears her cousin burst into loud sobs.

"I thought with you there, I could depend on you," she says accusingly.

Rina's heart sinks. "I will call you in a short while," she says and hangs up. 'May be Chandni had not left' the thought flashes through had not left her mind. It is confirmed when a middle-aged aunt comes running toward her and says, "*Arey*, Rina. I am sorry. I forgot to tell you that I took the car for some important errands and I told Chandni I will be back soon. Where is she? I have been looking for her. She can leave now."

Rina resists an urge to slap the rotund, unthinking,

uncaring, selfish woman. To think of herself first and not about the bride's, her own niece's need! But there is no time to lose or else bedlam will take over. "Stop it," Rina screams at the horrified woman, pushes past her, running to different rooms, searching. Desperately she over turns various bundled comforters, mattresses, lying strewn across the floor. She even looks under the beds.

No sign of her niece.

Ashok appears. Rina vanishes to the terrace. She does not want to scare him, not yet. He looks harassed enough. She must think. She stands quiet for a moment, to catch her breath, looking down at the road, at the relentless traffic and overwhelming crowds when suddenly, she hears gentle snores. She turns around and makes her way to the distant corner of the huge terrace. There in a corner, cocooned under a rough blanket, sleeping on the hard floor is her, elusive niece. Rina smiles. The poor girl is unaware of the many impending heart attacks she would have been responsible for, if she had not been found in the next couple of minutes.

The phone rings. Rina knows it is her cousin. She is hyperventilating. "Have you been able to find her? I just got Ashok on the line."

"Yes," replies Rina calmly. "She is here. I am bringing her home."

Ashok appears and gives her a hug. "You are our heroine! You saved the day! Thank you, my pretty sis-in-law."

Rina sees Sharad, her husband walk into the flat. She has missed him. He smiles and waves. She runs into his arms. It is party time.

***

The next day begins with the first of the many no-expenses-spared, lavish wedding functions. An evening of cocktails and *Sangeet*, an occasion of non-stop dancing to the accompaniment of music by one of Bollywood's famous singers. It must have cost her brother-in-law an arm and a leg.

Finally, arrives the grand finale, the much awaited wedding to be followed by the grand reception. At least a thousand people are invited. All the who's-who of the city are present. Rina is already exhausted and she can feel her adrenaline plummeting. But, she knows her cousin sister and her husband depend on her and she must not let them down.

Fondly, Rina watches her niece Chandni and her Prince being joined in a happy union. She throws rose and marigold petals on them. The two are truly a made-for-each-other couple!

She looks around and watches the guests busy eating, chatting, merry making. Weddings are like that!

The melodious sound of the *shehnai* fills the air. She drags Sharad, her husband towards her brother-in-law. On the way she picks up a tall glass of chilled juice from a tray being circulated by a uniformed waiter. She hands it to Ashok who looks at her thankfully, with a look of relief in his eyes.

The DJ now enters. It time for non-stop dancing. The fun has begun.

Sharad and Rina dance to the thumping beats being belted out. Her cousin and her husband join them. The bride and the groom walk in, soon after and give Rina a big hug. The camera flashes just then.

It is a Kodak moment! All is well that ends well, as the bard would say. Rina mouths to her husband and winks naughtily at her niece.

There is a commotion. "The bride's grandmother has fainted," someone shouts.

"Oh no," mumbles Rina, rolling her eyes, then sees Ashok,

her brother-in-law push his way through the thronging crowds, as though he was looking for something. On seeing her, a smile dawns on his face. He beckons to her with pleading eyes. Poor fellow, it appears she's the only person he can depend on.

"Go, my dear Superwoman, you are needed!" says her husband. "Poor fellow, with that weakling wife of his, you are the only person he can depend upon!"

Rina stares at him. That is a big compliment coming from her dear husband. Dependable! Wow! She blows him a kiss before making her way to the scene of action and quickly gets swallowed in the upsurge of the crowd around her.

28

Ketlo Majeno Chokro
(What a Nice Boy)!

Shenaz A. Setna

Dear Diary,

It's started again! Now my sister is married and packed off, I have become the focus of all the old biddies in our extended family and our neighbours of Dadar Parsi Colony! Ugh! Why can't they mind their own business? I suppose their daily lives are so humdrum and boring that sticking their beaky noses in other people's *masala* pots spices up their lives!

Do you know what Rhoda Muncherji did? Well, when I returned home from work a couple of evenings ago, I saw her chattering animatedly away with Mother. As I made my way to my room to refresh myself, I caught a couple of phrases, one of them being *"ketlo majeno chokro che!"*[1] which made me roll my eyes and chortle at the same time. When I entered the living room to greet them, they went silent abruptly. Rhoda hurriedly got up, smiled and greeted me with a slightly red face and scurried out of the door at express speed. My suspicions were aroused a bit, but as nothing happened for a few days, I forgot about it.

---

1 What a nice boy he is

Today, being a Saturday, I returned home from work around two in the afternoon, ready to have a nice home-cooked lunch followed by a snooze, before painting the town red with my gang of friends. To my annoyance, Mother requested me to help her for tea and then told me to be up and ready around 3.30 pm as guests were due to arrive by 4 pm. I thought that they were some of my parents' friends. My suspicions were aroused a bit again when Dad didn't go for his weekly bridge game and was dressed in a shirt and trousers, not his *sadrah*[2] and pyjamas–his and most Parsi men's usual weekend, relaxed, home attire.

Well, at 4.10 pm (I saw the clock) the door bell pealed. As mum ushered the guests in, I stood by the window watching them enter the living room. A middle aged Parsi couple and gasp! – a lily livered, pasty faced, thin as a reed, young man, with the most enormous walrus like moustache I had ever seen! I nearly burst out laughing, but my father's glare and expression brought my impulse under control. Mum wasn't far from laughing either; she kept smiling all the time with a silly expression on her face!

By now, I had cottoned on that this was a matchmaking set-up, when the doorbell rang again to admit a very "bustling with goodwill and energy" Rhoda. Introductions were made and then I helped mum serve the tea and snacks to the guests. Eventually I had to sit down, but the only chair available was next to the Walrus!

His slightly beady eyes eyed me up and down a couple of times and I felt a quiver of unease and revulsion shudder down my spine. He soon started asking me the usual questions in a deep gravelly rough voice that belied his status... not a good match.

---

2 parsi muslin undergarment

"Are you a graduate?" he barked out!

"Yes," I replied quietly.

"Arts I suppose!" he sneered. "No, Science actually, BSc.." again my tone was measured and quiet. "Really, what a waste of your time and a seat—you girls get married and take up a seat that a guy needs and could use well!"

I was fuming by now in horror and rage but before I could articulate a fitting response, out came the next cannon ball from his mouth. "And what are your hobbies? Apart from shopping?" he continued barking.

It was only the good manners and breeding inculcated in me from my childhood that prevented me from saying or doing something to him that I would or would not regret. This was like a crazy sitcom show on TV, so I decided to remain calm and play the part.

"I love to read and listen to music, I love the Beatles and Mozart" I replied in the best saccharine sweet voice I could muster.

"You must be a bookworm and an old-fashioned one! I don't read, except for newspaper headlines and stuff relating to work. Everything else is on the screen. Music bores me! I play cards, carom and cricket at the Dadar Parsi Gymkhana in my spare time! Do you play?"

"No, none of them, they bore me!" It was my turn now, I thought. "What have you graduated in?" I asked him.

He scowled at me before replying, "I told you I don't like to read. What's the use of studying those big fat books and then applying for some two-bit job? I work with my hands and for myself."

"So what is your line of work?" My annoyance and horror had slowly turned to relief. There was no way I could consider this male specimen seriously as a prospective life-partner and my parents would never approve of his lack of education, employment and prospects.

And then, he committed the final faux-pas. He slurped the remains of his third cup of tea noisily from the teacup, rammed the last of a large chunk of *bhakra* into his mouth and with his mouth full, literally spat and spewed out, "I fix radios, TVs, fridges, etc. and I earn about Rs.10,000 to Rs 15,000 a month." Bits of *bhakra* flew around him, some into his moustache and some into the air, visible to all around him. I recoiled hastily, and looked at my father with desperate eyes.

He swallowed the *bhakra* and then pointed to me with a long bony finger with a big hideous silver ring on it, he then and questioned my father. "And what does she earn?"

Everybody gasped, especially Rhoda who let out a high pitched shriek as well. Before my father could react, the boy's mother observing the worsening situation, said in a wheedling tone, "Why don't you two go out for a short drive? You'll get to know each other better, *ane aapre mota log jara vaat* discuss *karsu!*"[3]

He got up, dusted the crumbs off his moustache and clothes and asked me if I could drive and which car I drove. I nodded, and before I could proceed further, he announced that he was saving up for a Mercedes, even if it took him years!

Somehow, I couldn't move. Dad had recovered his wits but now was in imminent danger of losing his temper. My mother, graceful as ever, got up from her chair and politely offered them some more tea and in doing so beckoned me over. As she passed them by, she announced quite loudly, *"Maari chokri ne badhu aavrech- ghar nu kaam, bahar nu kaam, gani hushiyar che"*[4] and she pushed me into the kitchen.

---

3 We older folk will discuss things.

4 My girl can work both in the house and outside it very well, she's very clever.

She closed the door immediately and burst out into peals of laughter which she tried to muffle with a kitchen towel. I stared at her in total bewilderment. "Don't worry sweetie," she spluttered amidst giggles, "Do you think Dad or I would let you get involved with that *namuno* ? I didn't want you to even go for a drive with him, he's creepy but pathetic. You stay here, don't come out, I'll get rid of them!"

As she opened the door, we could hear my father, his loud voice barely controlled with suppressed fury; "I don't think they are well suited for each other. *Maari dikri ne puchi ne hamaro final answer aapshu.*"[5]

"*Tamara dikri ne puchso?*[6] Who is she to make a decision? You as a father have the final say and she has to obey you. We have brought up our children like that only!" his father snarled.

"*Maaro dikro ketlo majeno chokro che!*" exclaimed his mother.

At this, my father exploded! "And this father will ask his daughter, but we all say no! *Samjoch?! Chalo,* better *che ke tame amna jao!*" *(Better if you leave now!)* he roared loud enough for the neighbours to hear. He turned to Rhoda, who was looking aghast at the turn of events and for once rendered speechless. "Next time, *tame sochi, samji ne kaam karo! Aava *#*# ne na lauta!*"[7] he scolded the hapless lady. My father, nearly six foot tall and weighing around 200 lbs, advanced on the family who were still hovering around. mortified, they retreated and scuttled rapidly out of the living room, towards the main door.

My mother, as usual, had the last word. "*Arre Rhoda, aava sooko boomlo dudh pau kadko ne kai mara ghere lavi? Ene kejhe*

---

5 My daughter will be asked before we give our final decision.

6 You will ask your daughter? Samjoch means "understand?"

7 Think before you do things. Don't bring such unpleasant type of people.

8 Why Rhoda, did you bring such a dried up, pasty-faced, poor Bombay duck to my house? Tell him to remove his moustache, else how will any girl kiss him?

ke moochi kaari nakhe, koi bhi chokri mua ne kiss kem karse?"[8]
She gave a wicked snigger and laugh and banged the door shut
behind them. We then all collapsed on the sofa, holding our
sides and each other in love and in mirth!

My parents have assured me that I'll find my prince amidst
the frogs! So let's see what the next one is like!

And you know what, dear diary? I don't even remember his
name. I guess I'll always remember him as the Walrus! Good
night!

❏ ❏ ❏

Author's Profile

Rita Chhablani alternates her time between India and Chicago. A graduate in English (Hons) from Bombay University she contributed lead articles to The Indian Express and was a regular columnist for The Maharashtra Herald.

A popular yoga teacher in Delhi, she went on to publish her first book, "The Joys of Yoga."

Her second and recent one, "Despite Odds...Tales of Choices" has received rave reviews. Chicago Tribune, a leading newspaper of the Windy City carried an article on her. Sakal Times, of *amchi* Pune featured her in an interview and labeled her as a "Writer for a Cause." Radio One also did a talk show with her.

Having worked for UNICEF, she is a champion when it comes to the cause of education for girls. She devotes a lot of time as a volunteer teaching English to girls in various schools.

She is the co-founder of a highly active critique group in Chicago.

•••

Jayashree Dhillon has graduated with English (Hons), followed by a Post Graduate Diploma in Journalism, both from Pune University. She enjoys writing and has contributed articles to local newspapers since she was a young girl.

She has worked in an advertising agency and later, was part of a television project at the Film and Television Institute of India (FTII). This project was a joint initiative of the Govt of India and the UN. She has also been a sub-editor with a city magazine in New Delhi.

She has taught English and creative writing to children through the Newspaper in Education (NIE) programme, run by the Times of India. Thereafter, she taught English at the Symbiosis English Language Institute (ELTIS) for several years.

Now settled in Pune, Jayashree's stories borrow from her experiences as an army wife.

•••

Shenaz A. Setna graduated with honours in the science stream from St. Xavier's College, Mumbai and continued her education by obtaining a Diploma in Business Management from the Xavier Institute of Management, Mumbai.

Having worked in diverse fields ranging from the travel sector to the automobile industry, her first love was and continues to be the written word. She has sent frequent letters to various authorities and newspapers in connection with her being a member of the local mohalla committee. Shenaz is also a member of the Book club and currently on the committee of the United Services Library, the latter being located at the Poona Club.

•••

Manjula Shukla has a degree in management but has been following her dreams. Apart from a love of reading and writing, her varied interests are classical music and reiki. She is a yoga practitioner and instructor. She has been conducting creative writing sessions for children for quite some time. Here, children are encouraged to think freely and enjoy themselves. She is also a freelancer working towards development of children's textbooks and related study material.

•••

Mala Rihan has taken on new roles in every decade of her life. A qualified teacher and journalist, she has done copywriting, contributed to various magazines, taught in schools from Dehra Doon to Mumbai. She switched to corporate life with NIIT, starting as a counselor, then becoming a corporate trainer in the fledgling computer industry.

She began Phoenix, a career guidance and counselling centre in 1992, which was the first such effort in Pune.

An avid disciple of Paramhansa Yogananda, she spends her time writing, meditating and supports various social causes such as ARC (Action for the Rights of the Child), Poona Women's Council, Head Held High ...an initiative to educate and employ rural youth.

•••

Glossary

Aadhi – half

Achkan – Indian formal coat

Amavasya – new moon, a dark night

Ammi, amma – mother

Apa – respectful term of address for elder female

Arre, arey – used to express annoyance, surprise or interest

Ashram – hermitage

Ashtami – the eighth day of Durga Puja

Baba – father, to show respect for an elderly man

Babu – a respectful form of address for a man

Badimamiji – elder aunt

Badshah – king

Baithaks – sitting lounges

Bali kabakra - scapegoat

Baraat – groom's wedding procession

Barsati – roof top room

Bawa – slang for Parsi gentleman

Beta – son

Bewakoof – stupid

Bhaiya – brother

Bhaji – vegetable

Bhakra – a Parsi snack

Bhiksha – alms

Bibiji – mistress of the house

Boondi – a snack food made from sweetened, fried chickpea flour

Cha, chai – tea

Chaas – buttermilk

Chaat – savoury snacks

Chand ka dhabba – a blemish on the moon, which does not diminish its beauty

Chowkidar – watchman

Chutney – piquant sauce used as an accompaniment

Curry – vegetables with or without meat cooked with spices usually with gravy

Dadi – paternal grandmother

Dahi wadas – deep fried lentil dumplings served with yoghurt

Devi – one of the names for Goddess Durga

Dhansak – Parsi lentil dish

Didi – elder sister

Dhobi – washerman

Dosa – a pancake made from rice flour and ground pulses

Dramebaaz – drama king or actor

Dupatta – stole

Durbars – courts

Durries – Indian rugs

Fauj-i-Hind – army of Hindustan

Gharwali – wife

Guru – a Hindu spiritual teacher

Haveli – an old mansion

He Bhagwan – Oh God

Houda – carriage for sitting, placed on top of an elephant

Idlisambar – rice cakes and lentil curry

Jaan – life, a way to address a loved one

Jaanu – term of endearment

Jahaan – world

Jai ho – hail

Jai ho Maharajki – hail to the guru

Karma – the cycle of cause and effect

Khadi – homespun cotton

Khadau – Indian footwear

Khandan – family

Khansama – cook

Kheer – Indian dessert

Kutcha – crude or raw state

Kurta – traditional Indian dress

Lena-dena – take and give

Ma – mother

Maali – gardener

Maarodikro – my son

Mahals – palaces

Maharaj – king, head cook

Maharaja - king

Mamiji – aunt

Gur – jaggery

Mantra – a word or sound repeated to aid concentration in meditation

Masala – spice

Masi – aunt

Maska – butter

Mehndiwali – girls applying henna

Mundu – servant boy

Mojris – Indian footwear

Moksha - salvation

Moshai – the equivalent for Sir or Mr

Mutter poha – peas with beaten rice

Namaste – Hello, Indian greeting

Namuno – specimen

Nani – maternal grandmother

Nimbu-pani – lemonade

Paan – betel leaf

Paan masala – a mixture of herb, betel nut and sometimes tobacco

Paanwalla – person selling paan

Palang – wooden bed

Pakoda – fried Indian snack

Paratha – whole wheat bread

Purdah – veil covering the face

Puri – a small, round, deep-fried piece of Indian bread

Qila – fort

Raat-ki-rani – queen of the night, a fragrant flower that blooms at night

Raita – curd preparation

Raja – king

Rajai – quilt

Rajkumari – princess

Saali – sister-in-law

Sadhana – spiritual practice

Sadrah – Parsi undergarment

Sahib – Sir

Sambar – tamarind broth with lentils and vegetables

Samosa – Indian savoury

Sangeet – music

Sattas – cookies

Satu – a mixture of ground pulses and cereals

Shagun – good omen

Shehnai – type of flute played at weddings and other rituals

Sumo – Indian SUV

Tava – skillet

Thakur ghor – prayer room

Thela - cart

Tikki – potato cutlet

Trishul – 3 pronged weapon

Urad dal – a type of lentil

Zeera – cumin

www.ingramcontent.com/pod-product-compliance
Lightning Source LLC
Chambersburg PA
CBHW030546030726
47495CB00004B/1156